For S

Getting Away with

Murder

*****

Best wishes
Margaret
x x

M A Macklin

First published in Great Britain in 2021.

Chapter 1

Bridgeford-upon-Avon

Celia Bamford was intrigued. Who was the new arrival, the handsome stranger moving into Gallica Rose? He appeared to be alone – no sign of a wife or partner – perhaps she'd be joining him later…

Just the one car, very smart, a black BMW, registration number, JF 42.

A small, dark green removal van had tucked in behind the gentleman's car. Celia made a mental note of the company: Robert Gillingham and Sons, Coast Road, Eastbourne, Sussex.

She smiled, JF 42, how nice, I like a man with a cherished number plate…

"It must have cost a fortune," she whispered. "JF, I wonder what his first name is? John, Jack, Joseph, James, perhaps…"

Celia hurried across the room to fetch her spectacles – where were they? Oh yes, of course, she'd left them in the kitchen next to the toaster.

As she rushed back into the living room, she knocked her knee on the coffee table.

"Oh, damn! More haste, less speed," she announced, angrily.

It was alright, she hadn't missed anything. She spotted a few pieces of good quality furniture: a mahogany dining table, four matching chairs and a large, heavy-looking sideboard.

Celia scowled; the cream-coloured three- piece suite really let the side down – it revealed a distinct lack of imagination – taupe would have been far better…

"Still, I expect it will look quite smart, there's several dark beams in the cottage, it may need something pale to reflect the light."

Celia had been known to tell her friends that where décor was concerned, there was very little she didn't know. Colour-schemes, fabrics, carpets versus hard flooring, geometric patterned wallpaper, she always got it spot-on, well, in her opinion anyway.

Others might disagree and think choosing a deep purple wallpaper, in a dark hallway to be a very bad choice!

She returned to the kitchen – she may as well make another cup of tea – after all, she could be sitting in front of the window for some time.

When the car boot popped open, automatically, she looked up, craning her neck in order to get a better view but it wasn't easy. It was necessary for the vertical blinds to remain half closed in order to give her a degree of privacy or more likely, something to hide behind…

A large Italian-style coffee machine was held tightly by the man, this item received a further nod of approval.

"Oh, I say, we have a golfer in our midst," she murmured, as a bag of clubs appeared.

"I might need a few more lessons before I invite him to the club; wonder what his handicap is?"

Celia looked long and hard at the man's taut, muscular body. Watching him from afar prompted long- forgotten memories. She felt surprised by her lustful thoughts and suffered yet another hot flush!

After devouring a large slice of chocolate cheesecake (hoping to quell her desires) Celia examined his face: early sixties, perhaps? No more, surely. Quite tall, neat grey hair and even from a distance, she could sense he had a certain something.

Few men of that age would look so good in a grey-marl T shirt and tight designer jeans. Well, in Celia's mind they had to be designer jeans…

She picked up her laptop and typed 'cherished number-plates' into the search bar. After a few worthless efforts she came across a good match – two letters, two numbers: HB 94.

Celia became over-excited when she discovered the asking price – a hefty twenty-eight thousand pounds.

"Good grief," she whispered, "I could buy two really good cars for that! Anyone prepared to fork-out a similar amount of money on something so trivial must be extremely wealthy. He looks like a retired businessman, someone who loves to look smart and with a natural gift for charming clients and putting people at their ease."

She leant back in her reclining chair and tried to relax but it was impossible. She felt excited – seducing a man like that would be a huge challenge – nevertheless, she'd give it her best...

Celia had been correct in her assumptions: in fact, she'd been spot on...

Jim Foster, a widower, had owned and run The Foster Advertising Agency, based in Oxford. It had risen to the top, becoming one of the UK's best known and most successful companies. For over twenty years Jim worked like a Trojan.

Molly didn't complain about their lack of holidays or even Jim's twelve-hour days, she'd been a constant support. Molly had been his soul-mate and a wonderful wife.

Nevertheless, Jim had murdered her and felt no guilt. He'd walked out of her room and out of her life without taking a backward glance...

A feeling of undiluted jealously swept over Celia, her heart began to race.

Olivia Pendlebury must be absolutely delighted. Who wouldn't be with such an attractive man living next-door? How long would it be before Olivia sank her ruby-red, manicured nails into him?

Celia frowned, it wasn't fair, Olivia could have any man she fancied.

"Those of us who've been labelled plain or 'mousy' simply don't stand a chance. We're left with all the boring men, the uneducated men, the wimps or the men without money."

Celia disliked Olivia and everything about her. She hated Olivia's size ten pastel-coloured cardigans and her bloody cashmere jumpers, they looked perfect, as if made-to-measure.

"If I wore neat little cardigans," she whispered, "I'd end up look like a sack of potatoes."

Olivia was sixty-one but would pass for a lady in her mid-fifties.

Celia scowled. Yes, I admit, Olivia might be a widow too, but she's a very popular lady and never seems lonely or miserable...

Alan and Celia Bamford had been married for just under nine years when he packed a suitcase and walked out. He'd tried to be reasonable, tried to understand his wife's mood-swings and tyrannical behaviour.

On the day he left, Celia had been in a foul mood. She'd been prattling on endlessly about booking a world cruise but it was out of the question, they simply couldn't afford it.

"Wait until April, love, when my yearly bonus arrives.

"How do you fancy a week in Cornwall, in a five-star hotel? We can just about afford it. Remember that delightful hotel in Newquay, overlooking the sea? It's lovely down there, even at this time of year. We could certainly do with a break. Just think, cliff-top walks and for you, no cooking for a whole week! Go on, let me spoil you..."

Celia turned her back on him and stormed out of the bedroom, slamming the door behind her.

"There's just no pleasing you, is there?" he'd said, tearfully, as he walked through the front door for the very last time.

"You can have the lot, keep everything, I don't give a damn."

It had been no more than a marriage of convenience – two could live as cheaply as one. However, her constant criticism, nagging and expectations of a life far above anything he could provide, had driven a wedge between them.

For Alan, a new, longed-for life in the Lake District beckoned. Running a boutique hotel in this picturesque part of England had always been an impossible dream, a subject Celia would have refused to discuss, never mind consider.

Now, with Bertie Fielding (his best friend and lover) by his side, his dreams had been fulfilled. Two small rescue dogs completed their family. Alan Bamford had never been happier.

Celia had considered divorce proceedings, but having no idea where Alan was living, she decided to keep things as they were. One thing she ought to sort out was her will: she must write a new one – although Alan would remain her next of kin. She'd sent emails and texts but no reply was forthcoming. Perhaps, as soon as he walked out, he'd changed his email address and mobile number.

Bridgeford-upon-Avon beckoned; a lovely village and a good place to live. A change of scene and a few new faces might cheer her up. She knew the area well and besides, her only living relative, Uncle Reg, lived close-by in Burford. He was kind and gentle, not exactly a recluse, but a very private person.

Celia would visit him once or twice a month. She kept an eye on him, always taking a box of groceries with her, mainly fresh fruit and vegetables, she needed to know he was eating properly. Over the years, they'd become fond of each other and a good relationship had developed. Celia was like a much-loved daughter.

She'd managed to acquire a full-time job as a shop assistant, living in a small flat above the premises. Celia told anyone who enquired (including Uncle Reg) that her husband had died, tragically, whist working abroad. She felt unable to talk about him; her heart was broken into a thousand pieces. Sadly, she would never find another man like her beloved Alan…

In a strange twist of fate, the sudden death of Uncle Reg had been her salvation. A large, unexpected inheritance came her way enabling her to move up in the world.

Celia retired from her job in the newsagents and purchased a stylish house in the Evesham Road.

The move, further up the social ladder, made her more agreeable, for a while…

Her thoughts returned to the new, handsome neighbour – perhaps she'd try a charm offensive. She'd wash her hair and if she got a move on, there'd be time to add a few blonde highlights.

She'd wear a little mascara, something to enhance her small, pale eyes. The previous week she'd treated herself to a new lipstick, very bright, 'Pink Sensation'. Perfect for such an occasion.

Perhaps she'd bake a cake, such a cliché, so American, but he might be impressed. What should it be? A rich fruit cake or coffee and walnut?

"No, I think not. Let's have some cheese scones," she whispered, "men love them, my Alan couldn't get enough of them."

She shook her head as if trying to remove a mental image of the man who'd once been (and legally, still was) her sensitive, kindly husband.

Celia turned off her laptop, returning it to the small, pine coffee table. She gazed out of the window, straining her neck in order to get a better view.

"Oh, my God! What's going on now?"

She frowned; the front door was open wide. Olivia, looking as lovely as ever, stood before him. Just look at her, she's practically throwing herself at him. Oh, it's okay, she's walking away now, at least he hasn't invited her inside.

She felt smug. Fortunately, I'm not the one waiting for a hip-replacement. Yes, that'll slow her down a bit.

No bedroom antics for her!

Everyone in the village knew Celia's true personality: on the surface, all sweetness and light but underneath, cruel, spiteful and known to hold a grudge.

When she returned from the garden, holding a bunch of cut flowers, she noticed the removal van had left, she checked her watch, just after three-thirty.

I'll pop over now, before anyone else beats me to it. She looked in the mirror; the blonde highlights and make-up had given her a lift, she looked and felt ten years younger...

Jim Foster opened a couple of downstairs windows, encouraging the fresh, cool air to blow through. The cottage had been unoccupied for nigh on two years and although a little musty, there was no smell of damp or anything else that need cause concern.

He was aware that buying a property built in the 18th century could be inviting problems but he'd paid for a five-star survey which had given him peace of mind.

Jim's thoughts turned to Olivia, such a pleasant lady, very attractive too. He was sure they would be good neighbours and yes, company for one another.

He certainly wasn't looking for a deep, meaningful relationship. After his 'problems' in Eastbourne, it was the last thing on his mind. However, he wouldn't say no to a bit of fun! He'd been crazy about Georgia de Vere, loved her, desired her, far too much. She'd made him act irrationally, foolishly, then, when things went wrong, she refused to forgive him. He must put her out of his mind. He was starting a new chapter in his life, village life, would it suit him, would he fit in?

"Yes, of course it'll suit me, so many widows just ripe for the picking…"

Jim examined his reflection in the hall mirror and nodded.

"Yes, James my boy, you've still got it!"

Where women were concerned, he was like a magnet. He knew how to play the game, some women liked to flirt and if that was what they wanted, that's what they got. Others, more demur, preferred to play the waiting game but no matter, Jim always got what he wanted – in the end.

Just days after Molly's devastating stroke, Jim was informed (in a kind and sensitive way) she would require twenty-four-hour care, not just for a few months, but for the rest of her life.

After visiting his solicitor in Eastbourne Jim had driven slowly into Hastings, he'd needed to clear his muddled head. He'd parked outside a row of smart Edwardian villas, his eyes drawn to one of them: *St Christopher's House,* residential nursing home.

Looking back, he realized how fortunate he'd been, everything had slotted into place as if preordained by some higher power...

Due to the untimely death of their youngest resident (a mere fifty-one) Jim was able to secure a delightful room in this well-appointed nursing home.

St Christopher's House had once been a highly desirable property boasting a much sought-after sea-view. Great care and expense had been invested in order to re-vamp and restore the building to its former glory.

Before her devasting stroke, Molly had been so excited; her long-held dream was about to come true – a brand-new bungalow by the sea. Goodbye Oxford, hello Eastbourne...

She'd spent hours choosing carpets, curtains, a superb designer kitchen and a host of luxury bathroom fittings.

They'd been counting down the days. Molly would smile at Jim, her expression almost child-like. She'd look at the calendar and with a red pen, ticked off yet another day...

Playing the role of 'devoted husband', Jim had driven from Eastbourne to Hastings every single day, just to give Molly her lunch.

He was much admired by all the staff.

After Molly had eaten (hardly enough to keep a sparrow alive) he'd wait for half-an-hour or until she fell asleep, thus giving the impression he was reluctant to leave her side.

Jim lapped-up the kind words and empathy dished out by well-meaning members of staff.

Once home (and after a short nap) his afternoons turned into a routine-like performance. An hour's gardening or a brisk walk – followed by a ready meal, takeaway or poached eggs on toast.

Most evenings seemed endless unless the television provided him with an interesting documentary, riveting film or some form of escapism…

Jim's life had become tedious but tolerable until the day he met Georgia de Vere. Despite his wealth, charisma and good looks, the thirteen-year age gap worried him; Georgia might be spirited away by a younger man. They must get married without delay.

Killing Molly had been easy, surprisingly so. One day, chosen at random, when the staff were taking a well-earned rest, he'd placed a snowy-white pillow over her face and pressed down with all his might. Her thin arms tried to push him away. Ten minutes later it was over – she was dead.

Jim rearranged her arms, carefully, into a more relaxed position. He tucked a small floral cushion behind her head, positioning it to suggest she'd turned to look out of the window. Maybe she'd been hoping to catch a glimpse of the happy holiday-makers, especially the young children, as they walked excitedly along the sea-front.

Jim walked out of Molly's life without a second thought. There would be no feelings of guilt or remorse...

It would seem, to those that found her, Molly had passed away, all alone, but very peacefully.

"Not a bad way to leave this world," the doctor had whispered, speaking kindly towards the young carer who was becoming tearful. Molly had been much loved by all members of staff...

No post-mortem had been required or even suggested. Doctor Stevens had been gullible in the extreme: he'd signed the death certificate without raising an eyebrow. Cause of death: 'Heart failure due to complications after a prolonged bout of Influenza.'

As far as Jim was concerned, Molly had become an embarrassment; he hadn't wanted anyone to see the pathetic creature she'd become. Besides, she was holding him back, with expert care she might survive for years. Perish the thought! Jim decided he deserved a better life, more fun and a fulfilling sex life too.

Even before he'd murdered her, he'd informed their small group of friends back in Oxford and his sister, Mary-Jane (living in Australia) that Molly had died – influenza and complications after another massive stroke.

The funeral had taken place, a very quiet affair, Molly would have wanted it that way…

Chapter 2

A nine-day wonder

Celia took a deep breath: she must remain calm. She had a tendency to say too much when nervous…

She gazed at the cheese scones – yes, the tops were golden brown – they looked delicious. She selected four (with the best shape and colour) put them onto a small floral plate, then covered them with cling-film.

Jim was relaxing in front of the open patio doors when the doorbell rang, twice, with a real sense of urgency.

Perfume, wafting over him from a blood-red climbing rose was so intense, so exotic, he'd been lulled into a deep, much needed dreamless sleep.

Jim had endured a restless night in his brand-new bed. For many people, the first few nights in a strange property seem unnerving and promote thoughts of a previous dwelling and even a tinge of homesickness.

Jim tutted, shaking his head as he walked towards the front door.

A small face with lank hair and beady eyes was staring through the frosted glass: who the hell was it? Someone collecting for charity? Oh, please, not another Jehovah's Witness! Jim clenched, then unclenched his fists.

Celia jumped when the door opened.

"Oh, hello, I do hope I'm not disturbing you, I'm Celia Bamford from across the road. I made too many cheese scones and I thought you might like some."

Jim took hold of the plate and examined the scones…

He knew the advantages of showing good manners (especially when talking to a lady) they'd been drilled into him whilst attending a famous (and very expensive) public school. These lessons had not been in vain.

"Well, Mrs Bamford, they look absolutely delicious. I've always been very fond of cheese scones – how did you guess? Oh, even better, they're still warm!"

Jim smiled, revealing teeth that would not embarrass a man half his age.

He'd always been most particular, almost obsessive, about his appearance; even when gardening he'd wear a freshly laundered check shirt and a pair of smart jeans.

His olive-green gardening boots were a well-known brand, bought and adored by the landed gentry and the Royal family.

He took a step back, "Would you care to come in?"

Celia's cheeks were flushed, it was her lucky day. She rushed through the front door in case he changed his mind. The scones were placed on a small side table.

"I must say it looks rather lovely in here, no-one would guess you've only just moved in.

"Oh, by the way, you must call me Celia. I've been awfully busy today, however, I did notice the removal van, just as it was leaving. Are you a local man?"

"No, no, I've been living in Eastbourne for a few years and prior to that, Oxford. So, in a way, I've come back to my old stomping ground."

Celia smiled, shyly.

"Eastbourne? How interesting. Well, I can only say Eastbourne's loss is our gain. What brought you to Bridgeford?"

"I've always loved the Cotswolds so I drove around for a while and quite by chance, noticed the agent's board outside. It's rare to find a property like this on the market so I decided to snap it up!"

"Doctor Braithwaite lived in Gallica Rose for many years – such a charming, attractive man. Aren't we lucky? He's been replaced by another gorgeous chap!"

Celia giggled, like a besotted schoolgirl. She knew she'd gone over the top and said far too much but she didn't care, she must make an impression on this man before any other ladies in the village fell madly in love with him!

"Actually, you'll find us a very tight-knit community. There's always something going on. Are you interested in acting? You've certainly got the looks. We put on two shows each year, murder mysteries, that sort of thing and sometimes, a pantomime, just after Christmas. You might be asked to play Prince Charming."

Celia looked at Jim, she blushed profusely, he felt embarrassed.

Bearing in mind Jim's age, it was ridiculous to suggest he could play Price Charming and no less than a desperate sounding piece of flattery. Still, she was sure he wouldn't mind.

Celia had no idea how foolish she looked.

Jim was tempted to offer this unattractive lady a cup of tea but he knew her sort, he'd never get rid of her. Instead, he looked at his watch.

"Goodness, look at the time, I'm awfully sorry Celia, I'm going out in a minute, I have an appointment with my solicitor, in Burford."

"Oh, I must leave you in peace then," she said, trying to flirt with him, but sadly, lacking any necessary experience.

Jim was relieved to shut the door behind her. I suppose my 'history' will be broadcast all over the village; still, I needn't worry, I'll be no more than a nine-day wonder...

Chapter 3

Temptations

Celia couldn't wait to visit the Lovegrove sisters, identical twins, Alice and Ruby.

Dressing identical twins in brightly-coloured matching outfits looks cute – when they're young. However, a couple of middle-aged ladies keeping up this pretence, this unnecessary habit just didn't feel right – in fact one or two customers thought it was creepy and kept away...

Every six weeks their thick wiry hair would be trimmed into the style they'd worn since their teens and when a few unwanted grey hairs appeared, it was at more or less the same time. A pretty silk ribbon (pink or yellow) was tied into a bow then clipped firmly into their hair. Their domineering mother had insisted – little girls should always have a bow in their hair.

When the twins ventured out of the village (which was a rare and noteworthy occasion) heads would turn, but not with admiration. People stared at them and made spiteful comments…

Ruby had a large, unsightly scar on her left arm, just below the elbow, the result of cycling too fast down a steep hill and crashing into a gravel driveway. She'd been thirteen at the time.

The twins' daring idea (to set-up and run an upmarket cake shop) began as no more than a pipe-dream, but now, 'Temptations' was part of village life and had been so for over twenty years. This popular cake shop was known for producing food of a very high standard. Customers were willing to travel for miles in order to sample the Lovegrove sisters' famous dark chocolate cheesecake or choose something less calorific from their huge variety of vegetarian quiches.

At the rear of the shop four small tables had been covered with wipeable, red and white check cloths and when available an arrangement of fresh flowers was placed in the centre, adding perfume and interest. It was rare to enter the premises and find a table unoccupied. The ladies' reputation for making excellent coffee had spread and now Temptations was a stop-off point for weary salesmen.

Situated opposite the church, village green and next-door to Amy's Antiques, the shop was a hive of activity.

Sadly, the ladies had been unlucky in love, spurned at the last moment by fiancés who'd discovered (once married) they'd be expected to help out in the shop, especially on Saturday mornings. Not only that, they'd have to come to grips with a rather temperamental coffee machine!

The young men in question, Nick and Jeff, discussed this matter privately, coming to the conclusion that life behind a shop counter was not, and never would be, for them. Not likely, they'd had a lucky escape! Besides, Saturdays were set aside for fishing. Nick and Jeff were founder members of 'The Jolly Boys Angling Club', the twins must accept it, some traditions weren't optional – they were almost sacred.

Alice and Ruby made a bold decision, if men refused to do as they were told, they were too much trouble.

Their feelings of regret (for the life they so foolishly turned down) were eased somewhat by the warmth and affection shown by the majority of Bridgeford's residents.

Baking delicious cakes and pastries seemed more like a hobby than a way of making a living. Sadly, far too many cakes were devoured straight from the oven and long before they could be displayed in the shop window. The ladies were forced to make an extra tray of apple turnovers just for themselves, otherwise there would be nothing left to offer their much-appreciated customers.

After a busy day in the shop, Ruby and Alice had been known to devour four apple turnovers (each) before the six o'clock news had finished! Yes, the ladies were greedy, very greedy. Over the years their weight had increased to a rather alarming seventeen stone. Their XXXL pink and white check tabards looked ready to burst at the seams.

Alice and Ruby felt bitter and resentful. They enjoyed the company of men but since they'd 'piled on the pounds' their chances of meeting Mr Right were not looking good. Perhaps they would be stuck with each other forever.

Few women reach their early fifties without losing their virginity; however, the twins managed to achieve this dubious accolade with very little effort.

Dave Wallis, local electrician and huge fan of the twins' steak and ale pies, flirted with them, teased them, but which twin did he prefer? Occasionally, the ladies became snappy with each other, but only after one of Dave's visits…

Dave loved big women, the bigger the better. The twins reminded him of the naked, buxom ladies painted by Dutchman, Peter Paul Rubens, who'd died in the seventeenth century.

He'd seen Ruben's work, just the once, on BBC Four. He'd intended to watch the golf on another channel (a pro-celebrity match from Florida) but it was cancelled due to a thunderstorm.

He'd smirked, almost childishly before telling his mates about the programme. It didn't take much to set them off – he'd soon be getting a few sexist remarks.

"Guess what I watched last night? Only BBC Four, yeah, nothing else on. Some poncey arts programme, all about nude women."

"Yeah, I'll have some of that!" shouted Ted (one of the plasterers) causing a ripple of laughter. Dave received further lewd comments and more encouragement. By now, most of the young men on the building site had downed tools and walked over to join him.

"Turned out to be a flippin' rip-off, no more than a couple of toffs, yapping away, trying to out-do each other. Still, I got to see quite a lot of nude paintings and I learned a bit about art…"

Nothing happened in Bridgeford without the Lovegrove sisters' knowledge and quite often, their displeasure. The list of things of which they disapproved seemed endless and ever growing:

Anyone over forty wearing denim jeans, failure to attend church on Sundays, stilettos, pierced ears, tattoos, false eyelashes, trainers (unless black or navy), foreign travel, caravans, motor-cycles, snakes as pets and finally, authors who were brave enough to publish their own books.

Celia hurried along the High Street, breathless and eager to visit her friends.

"Oh, Alice, bring me a cup of coffee, please. None of that foreign stuff with a fancy name – just an ordinary one with milk. I'll have a fresh cream éclair too."

"Are you alright, love?" enquired Alice, ready and eager to hear Celia's news, "You look ever so flushed."

"No, I'm not – I'm in a right state. We have a new man in the village, you should see him! He's so handsome I thought I might die."

Ruby strained to hear their conversation. She was in the middle of serving an elderly gentleman who was buying four sausage rolls. As she stared at Celia, enthralled, a sausage roll missed the paper bag altogether and landed on the floor. She apologised.

'Oh dear, sorry. What am I like? Don't worry, the birds can have that one."

After the gentleman left, Ruby brought over a cup of coffee and joined her sister and Celia at one of the small tables.

"This better be good, Celia, look what I've just done."

She pointed towards the sign on the shop door.

CLOSED

back in fifteen minutes

Celia laughed, drank her coffee then wolfed down the éclair. Time was of the essence.

"Early sixties, I would think. Grey hair, tall, slim, muscular. Oh, those deep blue eyes, almost hypnotic."

By now she had the twins' undivided attention. They looked mesmerized, trying desperately to imagine this vision from above.

"So charming," added Celia, nodding her head. "He's called Jim Foster."

Just mentioning his name made her legs turn to jelly.

"As luck would have it, I'd just made some cheese scones so I thought, why not take a few over? Oh, silly me, I forgot to say, he's moved into Doctor Braithwaite's cottage, Gallica Rose. He invited me in, I said no at first but he insisted, practically dragged me inside."

Alice looked thoughtful.

"Surely there's a wife somewhere on the scene, or a partner? Men like that are never alone for long."

"No, Alice, honestly, there wasn't a glimpse of anything feminine. No photographs either, none at all, I had a sneaky look round. Perhaps he hasn't had time to put them out. Oh, just the one car, a black BMW, cherished number plate too, JF 42."

The twins were eager for more information so Ruby brought over another mug of steaming coffee and placed it in front of Celia.

"No, no, it's on the house," she said, when her friend offered to pay.

Celia sat quietly, not sure what to divulge next.

Is that it? wondered Ruby. She can't have finished, already, there must be lots more to Jim Foster's story. It felt like twenty questions, what should they ask next?

"Um, I know – is he local?" enquired Ruby.

"Oh, no, he's from Eastbourne. It all seems a little odd to me. Why move back to this area when you've retired to the coast? He's hiding something, I could tell. I was tempted to ask if he was married but you know me, I never pry."

Celia enjoyed being in the limelight.

"Guess what I said to him? 'Eastbourne's loss is our gain'.

'Oh, Celia," he said, *"you're a very naughty lady',* then patted my knee!"

Celia's tales were always embellished and far more exciting than the real thing.

"I wonder if he's a bit, you know…" murmured Ruby, with a knowing look in her eye.

"Whatever do you mean?" asked her sister.

"Come on Alice, wake up, you know very well what I mean. That type of man always looks immaculate."

Ruby turned to Celia, "Does he look gay? A bit camp, maybe?"

Celia sniggered, "Flippin' heck, Rubes, you must be joking! No way, I've never been more certain of anything in my life.

"Jim Foster is not gay – I'd bet my house on it. I'll have to do some more digging, see what I can find out. Meanwhile, if he pops in here, you'll recognize him straight away. Try not to faint. Remember, girls, I saw him first!"

After promising to let them know immediately should there be any further developments, Celia set off for home.

The black-and-white sign on the shop door was turned back to *OPEN*. They were ready, perhaps eager, for another batch of satisfied customers.

A large tray, displaying eight individual Bakewell tarts was added (by Ruby) to the attractive window display. The smell rising up from the warm buttery pastry acted like a lure for most of their loyal customers and indeed, anyone else with a sweet tooth who might be passing the open door…

Two weeks later, back at The Elms, Evesham Road, Celia settled down to watch the six o'clock news. A rather pathetic little meal consisting of two fish fingers, peas and a handful of oven chips was balanced precariously on her lap.

A dark grey Audi Q3 pulled-up and parked neatly outside Gallica Rose.

A young man opened Jim's wrought iron gate, passed through, then closed it behind him. A few glossy brochures were held tightly in his hand. Celia thought he was extremely handsome; he had a Mediterranean look about him: dark wavy hair and olive skin. Always bored and frequently lonely, Celia would find any man of that age attractive.

She nodded her head approvingly, yes, very tight pale blue jeans (without ripped knees) and an even tighter T shirt were most becoming.

Jim Foster appeared, a warm smile upon his face. He was a man who expected and appreciated punctuality.

"Ah, well done, perfect timing."

The two men stood together, just inside the gate, chatty away merrily – there appeared to be an instant rapport between them.

Celia's large living window was wide open enabling her to catch Jim's deep, sexy voice as it carried across on the breeze. Naturally, only snatches of their conversation could be heard and absorbed.

"I must say, Mateo, you have a rather splendid surname. Verdi, don't suppose you're related to the composer?"

The young man laughed.

"Wish I was, Sir, I might have inherited a fortune. Yes, Verdi wrote some cracking operas! Sadly, I'm not musical, I can't even sing in tune. It's quite a common surname in Italy. Actually, I was born in London, I'm an East End boy, fifth generation.

"You ought to see my uncle, Antonio Verdi, he's not a man you'd want to mess with. We tease him, he's got the look alright, he ought to be in the Mafia!

"Anyway, Mr Foster, enough about me.

"Many thanks for your email and to answer your query, in your position I'd think seriously about getting one. You won't go far wrong – the ladies are up for it – they say it rejuvenates them! Trust me, you'll have ladies queuing round the block. Yeah, even my mum wants one, she's about your age. My dad thinks they're stupid, just a gimmick. Still, if it works, why not? That's what I say!"

Both men chuckled in a rather juvenile, matey sort of way. Mateo Verdi followed Jim into the hall – the front door closing swiftly behind them.

As Celia leant forward – straining to see what was going on – the plate slipped out of her grasp, much of the contents landing on the floor. A dozen or so peas landed on top of her pink, fluffy, slippers; she shook them onto the carpet.

"Oh, blast," she shouted, "not now – not when things are getting interesting!"

She sighed, thinking, it could have been worse. Good job I didn't make pasta, what a mess that would have made. My tasty tomato sauce would have stained the carpet...

Celia's meal, now ruined, was swept up with the dustpan-and-brush. She rushed into the kitchen, throwing it, with gusto, into the pedal bin. Grabbing a packet of cheese and onion crisps she returned to the living room.

Using her small, bird-watching binoculars, she focused on Gallica Rose. There was no sign of either man which meant they must be in the dining room, kitchen, or upstairs.

Upstairs? Goodness me, what's going on? Was Ruby correct, Jim Foster, gay?

Just as the handsome young man was climbing out of his car, Celia was examining her watch. Once he'd left, she'd be able to say, confidently, he was only inside Jim's house for 'x' number of minutes. Would it be long enough for any *funny business?* She blushed at the very thought of it. What on earth had they been discussing? Sex, no doubt, men talk of little else.

'The ladies are up for it, it rejuvenates them. Even my mum wants one, she's about your age'.

Yes, that's what he'd said to Jim. I'd better write it down for the twins, it might be important.

Celia felt confused; their conversation had definitely been regarding women, although these days anything was possible.

The previous day, when watching breakfast television, Celia learned a new word, bisexual. Her upbringing had been very strict (a Catholic school for girls) and lacking in any form of sex education, which left her feeling neglected and rather too curious…

'*Even my mum wants one*'. Those words buzzed around inside her head. Whatever did the young man mean, could it be some sort of sex-toy? Perhaps they'd been planning an orgy! Surely not, the young chap's mother must be too old for that sort of thing.

She'd have to keep an eye open for any 'unusual looking visitors.' She'd hardly left her vantage point since the day Jim moved in.

Now that her suspicions were aroused, even Clinton (the bearded and highly tattooed postman) seemed a little effeminate to Celia. All was well until the day he mentioned, quite innocently that his favourite pastime was making and decorating fairy cakes. Celia was well aware Clinton was married with five children so maybe she was over-reacting…

If Jim Foster had been aware Celia was questioning his sexuality, he would have been mortified. Jim was and always would be, an alpha male...

He sat on the patio with a portion of chicken tikka madras, pilau rice and a large glass of white wine. The chicken was tender but the sauce, although hot, was bland and disappointing – no more than chillies and ginger. Where were the milder, aromatic spices?

Jim studied the brochures given to him by Mateo Verdi, the friendly bathroom fitter.

Despite Mateo's encouragement and highly suggestive comments, Jim decided against having a whirlpool bath installed...

What a pity Mateo's mum hadn't bought one of these fancy baths, if she had, he could have gone round to take a look, maybe try it out! No, buying one could be a big mistake then he'd be left looking foolish.

Any lady friends (using the new bathroom) might find a whirlpool bath too suggestive, would they be expected to try it out – on the first date? He sniggered.

"Take it easy Jim – everything comes to he who waits…"

He'd no idea there were so many variations of a fitted shower: free-standing, large, small, curved, walk-in or even placed neatly inside the bath – goodness, he was spoiled for choice.

Bushboard panels or very large tiles? Yet another conundrum.

Mateo was absolutely right – tiles look wonderful until the grout starts to discolour and the dreaded black mould appears. Bushboard, in a pale grey abstract design would be more serviceable. Perhaps he should invite Olivia round for a drink, she'd know about these things. A woman's eye for detail might be needed.

According to Jim, women could see the beauty in things that sometimes fails to register with their menfolk. Naturally, he would listen to her advice.

As Gallica Rose was a grade two listed building – heavily thatched and built in the 18th century – he was obliged to choose something with a classic design otherwise it would look out of place.

Mateo Verdi had recommended a Victorian-style bathroom suite, with an unsurprisingly grand name, 'The Prince Albert'. Yes, thought Jim, that's the one for me, it looks perfect. Let's see if Olivia agrees…

Chapter 4

Olivia's Story

Back in the day, Jim's sizable rear garden had been just over three and a half acres...

Long-time owners of the property, Colonel Rupert and Mrs Amelia Brookes-Ward had employed two full-time gardeners.

Jim was given this fascinating nugget of information (along with a few others) by local estate agent, Lenny Barnes, of Barnes, Hornet and Partners.

At some point in the 1930s, Colonel Rupert had been approached by a local builder who'd made him an offer he couldn't refuse. Would he be prepared to sell-off some of his land? The Brookes-Ward family (already very comfortably off) received a sum of money that if invested wisely would provide them with a very generous retirement fund.

Planning permission was granted for five luxury homes in the rear garden of Gallica Rose and also, one either side of this delightful cottage. One of the properties (to the right of Gallica Rose) was lived in now, by Olivia.

Due to the proximity of a small thicket, it had been decided the houses would be named after woodland trees. Jim's house would remain as it had always been, with a name, Gallica Rose, but no number.

These executive homes had been snapped up by professional men and women – working in Oxford – but wishing to become part of village life. Just forty minutes' drive from Oxford (known as the city of dreaming spires) the picturesque village of Bridgeford-upon-Avon became *the* place to live. Head teachers, high ranking police officers, NHS consultants and company directors vied with each other, determined to move to the village, put down roots and raise a family.

During the early 1980s, Olivia and Guy Pendlebury, newly married, moved into Broad-Oaks, 19, Evesham Road. Melissa Pendlebury had been born in 1985; she was artistic, creative and the image of her mother. Just after turning thirty, Melissa moved to California where she'd married a musician and settled down, enjoying a carefree life in the sun.

It had been a terrible shock for Olivia when she received an urgent telephone call from Guy's boss: she could remember every word. Her husband had suffered a massive heart attack, he'd been rushed to the Radcliffe infirmary, Oxford. Things were looking extremely grim.

Two week later, Olivia was arranging Guy's funeral.

The last few years had been utterly depressing. Although Olivia had made a few good friends in the village, she was desperate for someone to call her own, a man to embrace her and make her feel loved…

On hearing Melissa was pregnant, Olivia cheered up enormously. Once the baby was born, she would take a long, relaxing holiday with her family – who knows, she might not return!

She rushed round to tell Jim, who seemed less than happy. He frowned and looked at her suspiciously.

"I thought you didn't have any family."

He could remember Olivia telling him, on the very day he'd moved in, she was on her own. Maybe he'd misunderstood her when she'd said, 'no family to speak of' perhaps she should have added, 'in the UK'. He felt let-down, jealous: two pointless, childlike emotions.

Did he expect Olivia to fall for him, love him completely but love no-one else?

Jim Foster was a sociopath and a man with a huge ego – nothing and no-one could prevent him from getting what he wanted – especially where women were concerned. They must love him in return, but it must be an all-consuming love, no matter how many lies he told or how many people he hurt…

Chapter 5

Double Trouble

Dave Wallis was causing a rift, a serious rift, between the sisters…

Sometimes, when sitting down for a coffee or buying something nice for his tea, he sensed the twins were competing for his attention, possibly his affection too.

Dave was very fond of them; he found them attractive (in a rather quirky sort of way) but how on earth could he choose?

"Yeah, double trouble."

He couldn't really ask them for a date, not on the same day, that would seem unnatural, weird…

An image rushed into his head which made him laugh. Fancy sitting in the back row of the cinema with Alice on one side and Ruby on the other. When the lights went on – in the interval, he'd get a few strange looks! Perhaps he should toss a coin: many important decisions had been made that way. No, that would be silly, unnecessary. 'A' was the first letter of the alphabet, therefore, Alice would accompany him to the new Indian restaurant in Main Street, Burford. It could be embarrassing though; Ruby might be jealous and decide to follow them. She might behave irrationally – the twins had a certain reputation for being rather odd at times! What if she stood outside, peering through the window, pulling faces or glaring at them?

Dave laughed, he'd have to be straight with them, no subterfuge. They were so close they'd tell each other anyway...

He told them of his dilemma – there was no point beating about the bush – he'd take them out on a date, yes, but one at a time! Alice could have her Indian meal then Ruby, who'd expressed a preference for Chinese food, could go out with him the following week.

Ruby's brain was working overtime. What if Dave preferred Alice? She's quieter, more of a peacemaker, Dave might admire that in a woman. How could any man be expected to choose?

Physically, no-one could tell them apart, they'd tricked poor old Celia on more than once occasion. She didn't object. Afterwards, all three would sit down and have a jolly good laugh. What did Celia always say? Ruby closed her eyes, deep in thought. Oh yes, I remember now.

'Because you wear those gold lockets, you think you can fool the customers. Well, I'm used to your silly pranks, I know you swap them over. Ladies, you won't catch me out again!'

The lockets had been a twenty-first birthday present from Christine, a much-loved cousin who lived in Wiltshire.

Having a letter, 𝕬, engraved on one locket and a letter, 𝕽, on the other had been expensive because it was a time-consuming job. Christine had chosen well – insisting on a stylish Gothic script. Heart-shaped and made from rose-coloured gold, the twins were delighted with their lockets. Each morning, after they'd showered, the lockets were hung around their necks…

Ruby shook her head – oh my God, if Alice mentions Dave Wallis once more, I shall scream.

She walked into the bathroom, locking the door behind her. She would stay there for five minutes in order to cool down (she had to) otherwise she might say something she'd later regret. She needn't have bothered – Alice hadn't finished by a long chalk…

"It was the best meal I've ever had. Don't ask me what it was called but it sounded very foreign! Well, hardly surprising, we *were* in an Indian restaurant! Dave is ever so clever he knew exactly what to order."

Ruby couldn't be bothered to answer, instead, she turned on the television. She'd take a look at the BBC News channel.

"Did I tell you he's passed all his exams? Oh, yes, he can't go any higher. He must be a brilliant electrician. Despite being our age, he's going to start his own business soon, well, why not? If he does, he'll make far more money."

Alice went on and on for another twenty minutes.

"How about this, Rubes, he kissed me, honestly! Not on the cheek, either. No, it was a really long, passionate snog, thank goodness we'd both been eating spicy food!

"Wow, it made me feel all, you know…"

Alice laughed, almost hysterically, it sounded unnatural. She looked at Ruby and winked, not in a friendly way, it was more like a warning…

For a split-second Ruby felt nothing but loathing for her sister. Before tonight, Alice had never behaved like this – it made Ruby feel angry and jealous. Dave didn't kiss her in the same passionate way, why ever not?

Ruby checked her watch, eleven-thirty.

"I don't know about you Alice but I'm going to bed. I'm hoping to finish that book tonight, you know, where they move to Portugal, it's called, *'Another Man's Wife'*. The husband is killed by a drunken driver then she falls in love with a local man, a fisherman – it's ever so good. I do hope it has a happy ending! Anyway, see you in the morning. Sleep well…"

A week later, Ruby spent over and hour getting ready – her favourite dress, the black one, had to be discarded, far too tight. She was annoyed, the red one made her bottom look huge. Still, Dave must fancy her or he wouldn't have asked her out!

The Mandarin House was nearly empty, just two other couples. The man and woman spoke quietly, as if they'd important things to discuss. The teenager girls had already finished their meal but they sat there, laughing and whispering, in no hurry to leave.

Ruby felt nervous, unsettled. From the moment they sat down Dave monopolized the conversation and unfortunately, he'd talked about Alice and very little else. They were sitting by the window which helped, a little, at least she didn't have to make unnecessary eye contact.

"Alice was telling me all about your childhood. She said you've always dressed the same – bit odd isn't it, when you get to your age?"

"Well, not really," replied Ruby, looking and feeling extremely hurt, "we're identical, so we're used to it. I think the customers like it – we're a sort of novelty act!"

Dave laughed, warmly.

"Oh, I see, there's method in your madness! Let's order, shall we?

"Alice really loves animals, I could tell. I expect you do, too. I hear you've just got a Siamese cat, a chocolate-point. Such a pretty breed."

Ruby smiled, "Oh, yes, she's gorgeous, we've called her Blossom: she's about a year old, very affectionate. No-one knows where she came from, she appeared in the back garden one day and stayed! We've asked around, put flyers out in the shop, it's very odd. The problem is, she hasn't been micro-chipped so the vet couldn't help. We don't mind keeping her, we love her to bits."

"Yeah, I know what you mean. I used to have a dog, a Border terrier, lovely little chap. Had to have him put to sleep last year. I was so upset, I cried like a baby."

Ruby squeezed his hand, under the table.

"Oh, bless," she whispered.

Dave smiled, a very genuine smile, making her feel more relaxed.

The lights were low and romantic music was playing: 'Fly me to the moon' by Frank Sinatra. Dave leant forward, smiled again, then kissed her on the cheek. Did he noticed when she blushed?

Before she went to sleep, Ruby 'relived' the evening in great detail.

A slow start but once their food arrived, and after a couple of glasses of Sauvignon Blanc, things definitely livened up. She liked Dave, he was good company and more than that, she found him very attractive. Yes, his hair was receding and he could do with losing a stone, but so what? No-one's perfect.

His eyes were big and brown with long, dark eye-lashes, his teeth white and evenly spaced. When he smiled, he had a cheeky, boyish look about him. Was Ruby falling in love with him?

She sighed. The future certainly won't be bright, it could be messy, complicated, only one of us can win his love…

If she'd been invited back to his house, would she have gone, knowing what the outcome might be? More to the point if asked, would she have stayed the night? Yes, of course she would.

Suddenly, Ruby's heart started to race: she mustn't raise her hopes, he might prefer Alice, then she'd be left looking stupid…

Huh, if she invites me to be her bridesmaid, I shall refuse. Oh my God – I'd rather kill myself.

Ruby slept poorly; she had a tension headache. How on earth did they get themselves into this mess?

She removed two Paracetamol and caffeine tablets from their foil wrapper. What a pity Dave

Wallis wasn't an identical twin, that would solve all their problems...

The following morning began much like any other: a mug of tea and a plate of cereals followed by a quick shower.

Their entire life had been spent in Mulberry cottage, just a few doors away from the shop.

They started work at six-thirty, cheerful and full of enthusiasm. At the rear of the shop was a well-appointed, modern kitchen: planned and designed by the twins.

Every morning one of the twins would shout, *"Let the baking begin!"* It always made them laugh. They'd be millionaires if they'd been given a pound every-time they'd uttered these childish words!

Each new day was a challenge but they possessed such talent, such vision, things always turned out well.

Light, golden croissants, maybe a Victoria sandwich or two, sweet pastries, meat pies, sausage rolls (never a trace of gristle) custard tarts – it varied little from week to week. The ladies knew exactly what their customers wanted.

They drew the line at bread or even bread rolls – time consuming – bread could be picked up from any local food-store.

Children's birthday cakes were a speciality, you could have anything you desired. Nothing was beyond their culinary skills.

Chapter 6

Blossom

It started to rain, no more than a gentle shower, but enough to make Ruby rush outside and unpeg the freshly laundered tea towels and pink and white check tabards.

Blossom decided to rush in from the garden at exactly the same moment.

"Woops-a-daisy! Careful, my lovely, don't get under my feet. You nearly sent me flying…"

Dave was taking Alice out on Sunday, some sort of country fair; it was playing on Ruby's mind. The weather forecast was excellent.

"I'm so looking forward to it. First of all, we're going to Pershore Vale Country Park. Do you remember, Rubes, we went there as kids? Dad had that old mini, dark green, it's a wonder we fitted in. Good job our mum wasn't big like us. Still, neither were we, back then…"

The twins were quiet for a moment, sparing a thought for their dear departed parents.

"Anyway, Dave's picking me up at ten, we'll take a look at the fair, then have lunch at one o'clock. He's booked a table, somewhere special, he won't say where, it's a surprise!"

Ruby nodded, lost for words, what was she supposed say?

"You will be okay, won't you, Rubes? On your own all day?"

"Don't you worry about me, I can cope," replied Ruby, with a slight edge to her voice.

"I was going to make some marzipan animals for that little boy's birthday cake, you know, Jenny Wilkinson's son, Simon. He'll be seven. He wants lions, elephants, giraffes – stuff you'd find in Africa. I shall enjoy myself – I love being creative. You know that."

Once Alice and Dave had left for the country park, Ruby unlocked the shop door and turned on the lights in the kitchen.

She was feeling utterly miserable, almost tearful. What were they doing now? Had Dave squeezed Alice's hand as they drove along and gazed at her in the way only lovers do?

Blossom followed her into the kitchen, she sat on the floor watching as Ruby fiddled with colours, shapes and sizes. When ready, she fixed the tiny marzipan animals to the top of the birthday cake. She nodded, yes, perfect.

Ruby opened the fridge and poured herself a glass of wine. The bottle had been there for a couple of days, they should've finished it off.

It wasn't long before the bottle was empty.

The wine was kept for 'emergencies.' The sort of day when they'd been unusually busy or unable to sit down and take a short break. After they'd shut up shop and before they went home, a glass of Merlot would be enjoyed, sipped slowly, in a ladylike fashion.

Ruby stood up, feeling wobbly.

Blossom shot out from behind the kitchen table, a bright green catnip mouse clenched between her teeth. In her excitement, she narrowly missed bumping into Ruby's right leg.

"Oh, Blossom, you're at it again, you are a lively little thing!"

She giggled in a girlish way…

Once home, unwelcome thoughts rushed into poor Ruby's muddled head. We're getting to the age where a bad fall could result in a broken hip.

The bigger they are, the harder they fall.

She looked down at Blossom, purring contentedly on her lap.

"Oh dear, if I tripped over you, I couldn't get up again, not without help. It's not your fault, precious, it's us, we're not used to having a pet!"

Mulberry cottage was charming but quaint, with small windows and flagstone floors. They'd considered adding further carpets or rugs, giving a softer, warmer appeal, but so far, they'd progressed no further than a thick Oriental rug in the living room and a cheap off-cut on the landing.

A shocking image appeared in Ruby's head: Alice, in her nightie, standing at the top of the steep staircase, in the dark, tripping over Blossom...

If she fell down the stairs, she would scream out and bang her head on the bannisters. She might even break limbs when landing heavily on such a hard, unforgiving surface.

Would she be dead? Maybe...

"The bigger they are, the harder they fall. Oh dear, I must stop saying those nasty words."

However, if Alice wasn't dead, she could soon finish her off. A plastic bag placed over her head would do the trick. Alice would be in a state of shock, broken bones, perhaps, she wouldn't be in a position to fight back...

"Oh my God, what I am thinking?" she whispered, shaking her head, trying to rid herself of such a sickening image.

Moments later Ruby was smiling, a faraway look in her eyes, had she made a decision that would change their lives forever?

If Alice were to die, Dave Wallis would be hers, and hers alone, forever! They'd get married and live happily ever after, just like the loving couples in the novels she read with such passion and belief...

Accidents in the home are not unusual, especially in the middle of the night when people wander off to the loo, still in a dream-like state...

The table-lamp (with its dark red, dusty shade) was switched on at dusk, their mother had insisted upon it. The nearest streetlight, on the opposite side of the road, was too far away to bring any light into Mulberry cottage.

Once Alice was fast asleep (snoring loudly with the bedroom door wide open) Ruby would creep out of her bedroom and remove the light bulb: Alice would assume the bulb was no longer working. Excellent idea, although she must remember to put it back, immediately, after the 'tragic accident'.

Ruby nodded. Um, I shall say I have to wear ear-plugs, every night, due to the racket made by my sister, her snoring would wake the dead. Yes, she may have called out, after the fall, but I didn't hear a thing.

Blossom slept downstairs in the hall, her fleecy bed next to the night-storage heater. Ruby would admit, tearfully, the cat had been known to climb the stairs in the middle of the night. Some mornings, Blossom would be found at the foot of her bed or her sister's bed; they didn't mind, Blossom was warm and cuddly. It never occurred to them, not for one moment, dear little Blossom's night-time wanderings might be dangerous!

Ruby was getting a tension headache: planning a murder was totally out of character for a lady who could hardly be called, worldly-wise. She must make no mistakes – everything must run like clockwork. It would be Ruby who died, not Alice – she must get that into her thick head. From the moment she discovered Alice's dead body that was it. Goodbye Ruby. She would become Alice Lovegrove, not for the day, but for the rest of her life and no-one must ever find out!

Friends, neighbours and customers would all be saying the same thing: *'Oh my God, how awful. Fancy the little cat rushing up the stairs, so silently, just as Ruby was feeling her way across the landing'.*

It was jolly bad timing too. What were the chances of the bulb 'giving up the ghost' on such a dark, moonless night?

Ruby would look guilty.

"Oh dear, that bulb must have been in there for years. The last time it was changed, I bet mummy and daddy were still alive."

Alice's bedroom was in the back of the cottage. She walked past the top of the stairs each time she crossed the landing and hurried towards the bathroom – and hurry she did, the cottage was cold at night, no central heating, just a wood-burning stove in the living room plus a couple of electric storage heaters.

Ruby's bedroom was right next to the bathroom, she wouldn't be affected adversely by the loss of light. During rare but inconvenient power cuts, she'd been able to feel her way along to the bathroom.

Ruby would confirm (whilst dabbing her eyes) her twin had always been an untidy person.

She'd asked her sister, many times, to return the laundry basket to the bathroom and put away the numerous items left lying on the landing carpet (right in front of the bannisters) usually books, magazines or handbags.

Sometimes, dear Ruby seemed miles away – her head in the clouds – dreaming of the handsome male protagonist in her latest romantic novel…

Chapter 7

Turning on the Charm

Jim Foster needed a haircut; he'd planned to visit his usual barber before leaving Eastbourne but with it being such a busy time he'd failed to get round to it.

When questioned, Olivia suggested, *'Hair: by Shelly and George'*, a brother and sister who'd made a going concern out of a once derelict building. Situated opposite the Horse and Groom, the salon was bright, airy and very welcoming.

Jim waited no more than five minutes before his name was called. He smiled to himself, how he wished it was Shelly running her dainty fingers through his hair rather than her brother, pleasant though he was…

Shelly Barnes was in her mid-forties and recently divorced, she lived alone. She seemed happy (most of the time) her chosen career and friendliness towards her clients prevented her from feeling lonely. If she did have a bad day, well, she certainly wouldn't admit it to anyone. Besides, Jet, her faithful black Labrador would never let her down…

These and other snippets of information were passed to Jim by Olivia, who (unlike Celia) wasn't a lady who thrived upon gossip. Olivia was sensitive and perceptive: she'd discovered in her youth how the ordinary, mundane lives of those we meet can turn out, on occasions, to be quite remarkable!

Shelly and her brother, George Halstead worked well together. They decided to keep their partnership going despite George's recent marriage and subsequent move to Broadway twenty-two miles away. It wasn't a bad journey, unless it snowed…

He asked Jim if he lived alone: as always, he was ready with his sob-story. He'd acquired the knack of putting just the right amount of emotion into his voice: too much would make him sound an emotional wreck and might embarrass the listener – tears (from a man like him) would be out of the question.

A fine balance needed to be achieved.

The fact Jim had murdered his wife and felt no remorse seemed to have slipped his mind...

Jim loved to imagine the compliments left hanging in the air after he'd walked out of a room.

'Mr Foster is such a charming man and so good looking! He never complains but I get the impression he's lonely. He certainly hasn't let himself go, my goodness, he always looks immaculate.'

Jim smiled. No wonder men found him good company and women adored him! He replied to George's polite questions...

"Oh, yes, I'm all on my own now, I don't think I'll ever get used to it. We'd made so many plans."

Jim gazed into the mirror, admiring his reflection. George nodded and made appropriate comments as he worked wonders with a pair of scissors. Jim continued with his 'prepared' speech.

"I'd worked very hard for over twenty years, getting the business up and running, now it was Molly's turn. All I wanted was to spoil her and give her the holidays she'd been denied. We'd bought our dream home by the sea, but sadly, fate intervened – Molly didn't live to see the finished bungalow – it wasn't to be."

Shelly liked the look and the sound of Mr Foster – he was a *real* gentleman in the truest sense of the word. How sensitive he sounded, how caring! Such a sexy voice and deep blue eyes. She smiled, well, what's not to like? Despite the tragic and unexpected death of his beloved wife, he was determined to remain cheerful...

During the cold winter months, Shelly and her mum sat together (with a box of chocolates) watching movies from the 50s, 60s and 70s. Often in black and white, the acting somewhat 'wooden' but who cared? It was fun – pure escapism.

They loved the plots, the characters the stylish clothing and of course the glamorous movie stars. A few names popped into her head; Cary Grant, Steve McQueen, Paul Newman, Robert Redford, Gregory

Peck and many, many more. Yes, they were her sort of man.

She glanced across at their new client, um, Jim Foster wouldn't look out of place on her list! She caught sight of the clock; oh, heck, I'd better stop day-dreaming!

Her least favourite client, the dreaded Carolyn Fitzsimmons was having a cut and blow dry at eleven-thirty; if she was kept waiting for more than five minutes, she became quite scary. She had an expression that could turn milk sour...

After making three coffees, Shelly handed one to her brother and one to Jim.

"You look like a man in need of caffeine. Sugar?"

She smiled sweetly, putting her hand on Jim's shoulder then giving it a gentle squeeze. Jim looked up, surprised and delighted, was she flirting with him? Shelly was just the tonic he needed: warm, vivacious and wrapped up in a very womanly body!

Jim gave one of his charming smiles...

"You're right, dear lady, if I overdose on caffeine, it might do the trick. Oh, yes, sugar, please. I suppose I've been putting too much pressure on myself, it's quite unnecessary, there's no rush to sort things out."

More than anything in the world, Shelly longed to give Jim Foster a big hug: he was adorable...

Chapter 8

A Chance in a Million…

Jim turned off the television; he'd been watching a programme selected at random but already halfway through.

A Tour of the Lake District, with a voice-over by the popular (but over-rated) Liverpudlian comedian, Melvin Hepplewhite. Jim tutted – he wasn't impressed. Who the hell are these 'Z' list celebrities? They win some ghastly reality show then they're on our screens every evening. Before long they have their own quiz show, followed by a chat-show which nearly always turns out to be a disaster. Jim looked peeved.

"Oh yes, with my charm and good looks, I'd be the perfect chat show host; I'm really good at putting people at their ease…"

The programme had been a disappointment too. It looked more like a snazzy advertisement than a tour of the Lake District. Its aim was clear, to promote rambling, rock-climbing, cycling and other out-door pursuits.

Jim loved the Lake District, it looked spectacular no matter what the season and even from the comfort of an armchair. However, he didn't want the 'wrong' sort of people to start going there. Jim was a snob, although if anyone had dared to point it out, he would have denied it.

They'd driven to the Lakes on a couple of occasions (in the early days of their marriage) long before The Foster Advertising Agency took over his life. They'd discovered a delightful country-house hotel, quite by chance, a pretty setting and not overly expensive. Molly had declared it to be the loveliest and most unusual hotel in the whole of England...

He could visualize it now, surrounded by trees, oh, yes – there'd been a fast-flowing trout-stream nearby. The food was superb, Phillipe Barbeau, the French chef, providing everything you could wish for and more: coq-au-vin, scallops Provencal, boeuf en croute, choux pastries and French apple tart.

Jim shook his head, giving a wry smile. And the wine! He'd spent far more than he'd intended and certainly more than they could afford. They'd been given a room with a four-poster bed – a huge creation with emerald and gold velvet curtains – Jim said it looked Medieval. They'd slept on a goose down mattress and laid their weary heads on goose down pillows. He felt like Henry VIII and couldn't resist playing the part...

'Come hither, young wench. Keep not thy sovereign waiting! I shall make love to thee before the night is over...'

Molly had giggled and given him a hug. Of one thing she was sure, her husband was never boring.

Once they'd turned out the light, it was very dark (due to the proximity of the trees) Molly became a little anxious, hoping she wouldn't fall out of bed in the middle of the night or trip over a suitcase when she went to the bathroom...

These precious memories made Jim feel quite emotional. Molly had been a wonderful wife and he'd loved her very much.

He sighed, feeling sorry for himself. It's a pity she had to die – however, I had no choice, she was holding me back.

During their marriage, despite numerous offers, Jim had never strayed. He'd rarely desired another woman, that is, until the day he met and fell in love with Georgia de Vere…

"I've got it!" he said, loudly…

"Of course, the hotel was called The Cedar Tree. I can see the name now, huge black letters, written over the front door. I wonder if it's still there? Different owners perhaps, but I expect it's still in business."

He smiled as he turned on his laptop. I wonder if Olivia would fancy a short break? Everything above board, single rooms, no funny business. Just a little sight-seeing. However, I couldn't take her (or any other lady) to the Cedar Tree, it would feel like a betrayal.

"Oh, hang on, what's this? Boutique hotels – never heard of them."

So many to choose from. He liked the idea: friendly, quiet, attention to detail. Most of them catering for a small number of guests, three maybe four double rooms and a couple of singles, always en suite.

He'd scrolled through a few pages before his eyes were drawn to 'The Hidden Tarn', a delightful looking stone cottage – named after the mirror-like tarn, or lake, seen from the rear of the property.

The set-up reminded him of the home once owned by Beatrix Potter.

The décor looked attractive, stylish and welcoming; someone certainly had an eye for colour. The proprietors were a newly married couple: Alan Bamford and Bertie Fielding.

Such a homely photograph: one man with his arm around the shoulders of the other. They were perched on a dry-stone wall, presumably in the garden of their lovely hotel: relaxed, smiling, two dogs at their feet.

It took a while before the penny dropped. Jim shook his head, no, surely not...

Could it be him? Really? It was incredible! The same Alan Bamford? The husband of Celia, the man who had 'died' so tragically whilst working abroad?

Jim chuckled. This unexpected piece of information might come in handy one day. If Celia became a nuisance – spying on him, pestering him, interfering in his private life – it would certainly shut her up. However, he must confirm it was the same man.

Bamford had a nice English ring to it he could guess its origins, in fact the name brought back happy memories...

In his youth, Jim spent a week in the Derbyshire Dales, a cycling holiday with his cousin Josh, they were both sixteen at the time.

They'd visited Bamford on more than one occasion. They'd walked into the village pub, as bold as brass and despite being under-age, the publican had been more than happy to serve them. They sat, looking out of the window, each boy bravely consuming three pints of strong larger. No-one said a word, even though it was obvious to the regulars, they were unfamiliar with strong drink. Things were less rigid in those days. Unfamiliar with alcohol, they'd wobbled precariously when setting off on their bikes. A few locals (including the publican) had rushed outside to watch, laugh and applaud...

He'd find some pretext for seeing Celia, he might take her a little gift, anything that encouraged her to invite him inside. Would there be a photograph of Alan? Maybe, although if it turned out to be him, his reasons for leaving Celia would be something she'd want kept under wraps.

If a politician, celebrity or someone else in the public eye was found to be living a double life, Jim's late father would say, rather pompously: 'Nothing would surprise me about anyone!'

When Celia opened her front door, Jim had a warm smile upon his handsome face.

"Celia, this is for you, dear lady, I simply couldn't resist…"

He was holding a pot containing a Hybrid Tea Rose, its name, 'Celia's Delight'.

"I was searching for a rose to replace one that's obviously dead, preferably burgundy in colour. Anyway, as I walked away this lovely variety caught my eye, once I'd seen its name, I had to buy it. Pure white, repeat flowering and highly perfumed. Do you have room for it?"

"Oh, my goodness," replied Celia, her face pink with excitement.

"What a lovely thought. Do come inside. I'll put the kettle on, unless of course, I can tempt you with something else. A glass of scotch, maybe?"

She gave Jim a large glass of scotch, it must have been a double. She giggled flirtatiously as if suggesting (or more likely hoping) something of a sexual nature might be brewing between them…

She wondered if Olivia was standing by her living room window, if so, she might have noticed Jim walking through her front door.

That'll shake her up a bit, thought Celia, especially if she noticed the beautiful rose – wow, she'll be green with envy.

"Oh, Jim, would you care to take the rose through to the kitchen? It's gorgeous, I shall have to find just the right place for it."

Jim was hating every moment of this bizarre encounter but he managed to bluff his way through. Putting on a performance came naturally to him.

"Incidentally, Celia, did you know the Gallica Rose was grown by the Romans and the Greeks? Yes, it's one of the world's oldest varieties."

She smiled, revealing a row of stubby teeth.

"Oh, really? How interesting. I've always been passionate about roses, still, you may have gathered, *I'm a very passionate lady…*

"Dearest Jim, do come over here and sit beside me."

She patted the cushion on the tweed sofa. Jim could hardly refuse; nevertheless, he kept to his end of the sofa, sipping his whisky and biding his time. Celia gazed into his eyes.

"One can get awfully lonely without a man. I have friends, acquaintances, but it's hardly the same."

Celia moved a little closer, her voice no more than a whisper, she placed her hand firmly on Jim's inner thigh. Her eyes lit-up...

"The problem is, I miss the *physical* side of marriage, how I long to have a man in my bed: I've always had a very healthy appetite in that department."

Jim felt embarrassed, uncomfortable. He didn't appreciate hearing such comments from a woman he hardly knew and didn't find attractive.

However, had it been Olivia offering herself on a plate, her hand touching such a sensitive area, he would have found it very stimulating. He must change the subject and quickly. He moved his leg to one side, putting his knees together, her hand fell away…

"I believe you moved to Bridgeford after the tragic death of your husband. Am I right?"

Celia nodded and sighed.

"Yes, indeed you are."

She looked down at the carpet as if unable to carry on. Several moments elapsed before she continued…

"I moved here for a reason – so I'd be closer to dear Uncle Reg, my only living relative – born and brought up in Burford. A good man, a kindly man, but rather shy with the ladies…

"Over the years we became good pals but I didn't think for one moment he'd leave everything to me – that is, his house and investments.

"To be honest, all that financial stuff is way over my head. I intend to get a financial advisor to sort it out for me."

While Celia chatted away, merrily, Jim took surreptitious glances around the living room. At last – he spotted them – a couple of framed photographs on a small corner table. One photo was definitely showing a bride and groom, he could see an image of a long white dress. Was it them, a youngish Celia and Alan? It must be. If only he was wearing his spectacles…

"I really ought to be going, Celia, I have my burgundy rose to plant, I must get on with it, it's rather in need of a good soaking."

"Oh, what a pity, just when we're getting to know each other. How about another scotch?"

Jim laughed.

"I do believe you're trying to get me drunk! Do you know what I really fancy? A nice cup of tea, then I'll go straight home and plant the rose. Oh, by the way, it's called 'Queen of Darkness', a rather exotic name. Anyway, Celia, tea would be perfect."

Celia jumped up and hurried into the kitchen, she would do *anything* for this handsome man…

As she made a pot of tea, using her best china, she thought of Alan, but only because Jim had just mentioned him. Despite having heard nothing from him since the day he walked out, she assumed he was still alive.

Was Alan living with another woman? Maybe he'd become a father, oh yes, he would have liked that...

Celia had yet to change her will: doing so would mean accepting – finally accepting – her life with Alan was over...

She knew she'd been unkind to him, constantly belittling him, nagging him, making his life a misery. He was sensitive; he should have married a lady with a laid-back temperament...

Although Celia was out of sight, Jim strolled around the living room with a nonchalant air. He inspected a midnight-blue Moorcroft vase (decorated with sweet-peas) giving it a nod of approval. However, he considered a pale green soapstone Buddha to be cheap 'tat'. He replaced it on the shelf.

He crossed the room to examine Celia's vast collection of books. Dozens of glossy recipe books, a few Dickens, a thick ornithological reference book (How to identify British birds) five paperbacks by Ruth Rendell and six by Lesley Pearce. Just as he suspected, nothing out of the ordinary.

He'd passed the corner table twice, yes, there was no doubt about it, the man in the wedding photograph was the same Alan Bamford.

Celia (perhaps a little slimmer) was easily identified. Even then, with youth on her side, no-one would've said she was pretty.

Jim smiled to himself, thank goodness for ginger hair! In the charming, idyllic scene created so carefully by Alan and Bertie, Alan's hair was greying at the temples but still visibly ginger...

Chapter 9

Surprising Revelations

Celia spent a restless night, she felt disappointed and confused. Why had Jim reacted in such a cold and heartless way?

He'd given her a such a lovely present – a Hybrid Tea Rose, very romantic – he'd even chosen one bearing her name. She assumed he was giving her a subtle message, a coded way of saying 'I find you very attractive' or at least, 'I enjoy spending time with you.'

Perhaps she'd misread the signals…

She'd put her hand on his inner thigh hoping he might suggest going upstairs. He should have been thrilled to bits. She couldn't have made her feelings more obvious. Good grief, a normal man would become aroused but Jim moved away and his expression seemed anything but happy. Had he been offended?

After absorbing the childish comments made by Ruby and Alice it was no surprise her brain was in meltdown. Jim Foster – gay?

Celia had developed a rather unhealthy interest in other people's sex lives, especially the rich and famous.

She'd read an interesting article the previous week, confirming Rock Hudson, one of her favourite movie stars, had been a homosexual. No, he couldn't be, he'd been in love scenes with Doris Day – they looked so good together. Poor, naïve Celia; it took days to sink in. She'd assumed they were lovers in the real world too.

Rather than question Jim (face to face) which might receive a frosty response, she could always try to find out – thank goodness for the internet! He'd run his own business for over twenty years, perhaps she'd discover something interesting, a little scandal maybe. Very little escaped the eagle-eye of the internet…

Newspapers kept records and Eastbourne wasn't far from Brighton, a refuge for 'interesting and colourful characters.'

She turned on her laptop. Perhaps she'd come across a photograph of Jim at a Gay Pride rally! She burst out laughing, highly unlikely – Jim Foster, wearing rainbow-coloured trousers?

Celia clicked on the link: The Eastbourne Herald – Archives. It was a good starting point, she'd scroll back, five years should be enough.

As Foster is a relatively common name, dozens of entries appeared. Where to start? How about Jim's wife, Molly Foster? Births, Deaths and Marriages? Oh, no, silly me, Jim said Molly died when they were living in Oxford. Much to Celia's surprise, there *was* an entry for a Molly Foster! A notice had been placed by the manager of St Christopher's House, a residential nursing home, but no more than her age and a few kind words:

Molly Alicia Foster, age 62, formerly of Oxford. A sweet-natured lady who will be missed by the staff and her devoted husband, James. The funeral has taken place. Donations please to the British Red Cross or any wildlife charity.

Celia frowned. Had someone made a careless mistake and typed Eastbourne instead of Oxford? Impossible.

Jim's wife died in Oxford, I'm positive, yet here's Molly's name in the Eastbourne Herald. Jim made no mention of a nursing home. He'd looked quite emotional when he told me Molly hadn't spent a single day in her dream bungalow. Something doesn't feel right, what's he hiding? Why would he lie about something so personal?

Celia scanned through a lot of interesting articles but nothing concerning Jim Foster: the odds of finding anything else were stacked against her. Then, quite by chance, her eyes were drawn to something that made her pulse race...

Weekly Court Report - by Peter J Ryder

James W Foster of The Knoll, Eastbourne: Found guilty of breaking and entering.

Celia tutted. "Well, that certainly won't be my Jim."

Suffering from a nervous breakdown, due to the recent loss of his beloved wife, James W Foster acted totally out of character by breaking into the bungalow belonging to his good friend, Mrs Georgia de Vere. Several valuable items, including gold earrings, a solid silver carriage clock and an engraved Rolex watch (belonging to Mrs de Vere's late husband) were stolen. The bungalow was left in a state of disarray. When questioned, Mr Foster said he'd been looking for a book, 'The Fortune Teller's Handbook', which he believed had 'taken against him', suggesting he was dishonest and untrustworthy.

On one occasion the book declared Mr Foster to be 'surrounded by death'. He was terrified of the book which appears to be from the Victorian era. However, as it displays no author, printer or publishing house its origins are unknown...

Mr Foster claimed the book had a 'supernatural aura' and possessed the power to influence his life and the lives of those around him, causing misery and fear. He said the book should be destroyed by fire although Mrs de Vere has no fear of it.

The crime took place when Mrs de Vere was at the theatre with her neighbour.

Mr Foster, of previous good character, received a sentence of one-hundred-and-twenty hours community service. This would have been greater had he not pleaded guilty.

Mr Foster apologized to Mrs de Vere for stealing her property, ransacking her bungalow and for putting her through such an ordeal.

He felt his 'uncharacteristic' behaviour had been justified in order to cover-up the true nature of his quest. Despite his efforts, he'd been unable to locate the book as it had been left with Mrs de Vere's neighbour, a Mrs Pauline Bairstow.

There was a footnote to the article:

For over twenty years James W Foster owned and ran the highly successful Foster Advertising Agency, based in Oxford. In its hey-day, one of the UK's top ten companies with clients in the United States, Canada and most European capital cities.

Celia didn't have a drinks cabinet but she kept a bottle of sweet sherry in the kitchen cupboard, next to the whisky. Her hands were shaking with excitement.

She filled a mug, remembering to sip it, slowly. On one occasion, being unused to alcohol she'd knocked it back in one fell swoop, then regretted it.

"I was right all along," she whispered, triumphantly, "he *is* hiding something."

Jim Foster, a man with a criminal record, incredible…

Celia wrapped a thick cardigan around her shoulders, she must go and have a word with the twins. Should she print off a copy and take it with her? No, that would be quite unnecessary, they could look it up for themselves.

Once again Celia became light-headed; it would seem alcohol didn't agree with her. She ought to return to the living room and sit down for a while...

She awoke with a start, thirty minutes later, her head thumping. Once the pain-killers began to work, Celia was able to sort out her muddled thoughts. Before she rushed off to Temptations, she must decide if it was the best course of action. Did the twins really need to know Jim's dark secrets, right now? The answer was no, there was no great hurry...

She might drop a few hints first and see how Jim reacted. He would go into meltdown if he thought his personal life was being discussed in such a public place – a café, full of people? How awful! Anyone could be listening.

Celia sniggered. Imagine how embarrassed he'd feel if his precious Olivia was made aware of his strange behaviour. Jim Foster (Mr Smooth) a man with a criminal record!

She laughed. Oh boy, these revelations were like gold-dust. Naturally, she would 'warn' Jim that his secrets might be revealed – accidently or on purpose. For once, she would be in charge.

Alice and Ruby could never be described as discrete, not by any stretch of the imagination. It wouldn't be long before the whole of Bridgeford knew about Jim's shady past. The residents might stare at him or even laugh at him behind his back. Celia sniggered – he was a proud man – he would go nuts!

She'd invite Jim round for coffee and a slice of home-made cake. Once he was sitting comfortably, she'd explain what she'd discovered and just how far she was prepared to go. *Oh yes, the worm had turned...*

He'll have to be nice to me then, won't he? He'll soon be in my bed, making love to me. Oh my God, I can't wait...

Celia smiled, she was proud of herself, although she had to admit, her cunning plan was no less than blackmail.

Didn't she realise she was playing a dangerous game?

Her face felt flushed. There was so much to look forward to – Jim would spoil her – anything to keep her quiet! An expensive meal would be nice. Even the cinema would be a real treat if he was sitting beside her. She didn't care where they went as long as they gave the impression of being a loving couple.

Yes, but afterwards? What would happen when he drove her home and she invited him inside? He couldn't say no, could he?

How she longed for Jim's embrace. He was so handsome, so desirable. Perhaps a little cruel at times, but always, every bit the alpha male. Celia tried to imagine him, lying in her bed, their naked bodies entwined. This time, he would be stroking *her* thighs…

A shiver ran down her spine. Oh, yes, she'd seen it all before in films and on the television – she was well aware of what she was missing. Celia envied the women lucky enough to have a red-blooded man in their lives. One thing played on her mind – would

Jim be disappointed when he noticed her breasts were quite small?

She giggled. "Who cares? I'm sure lots of men are attracted to small breasts."

She mustn't get ahead of herself but nevertheless, the future was looking pretty good.

Perhaps, before she said anything to Jim, she ought to check out a few other newspapers. The Daily Telegraph and The Oxford Mail might turn up a few surprises…

Celia hadn't felt so excited since the day of her wedding. Sadly, their wedding night turned out to be a complete and utter disaster. Poor Alan was 'far too tired' to give her more than a goodnight kiss.

To admit they'd made love no more than once or twice a year would have been upsetting, but true. Her marriage had been a disappointment: nine wasted years…

Celia smiled, good gracious, the Daily Telegraph had been in existence since 1855.

Her search hadn't been in vain – in fact she was pleasantly surprised – there was a great deal of interesting information to be found on the archive pages, it would be very easy to get distracted.

She typed Jim's name in the search bar, intrigued by one of the top results:

Charity Auction

Two good pals raise over £250,000 for Children's Charity!

At the head of the article was a delightful photograph of Jim and Bernie P Epstein, neither man looked more than forty. The good friends had masterminded a charity dinner and auction at London's renowned Tudor Rose Hotel.

They smiled into the camera, looking as if they'd already had plenty to drink. Jim's arm was across Bernie's broad shoulders – this must have been a night to remember...

There wasn't a photograph or even a mention of their wives; Celia was disappointed, she longed to see an image of the late Molly Foster. Had Molly been beautiful? She knew the answer – Jim could have married any woman he wanted.

Suddenly, Celia was overcome by a feeling of sadness and despair – she felt as if a dark cloud was looming, high above her head.

Oh, dear, poor old Bernie P Epstein, I'd forgotten all about him. I feel awful now. I really enjoyed watching the adverts for his Princess Stores – you wanted to give him a big hug – he was one of the good guys. How could anyone murder such a generous and kindly man?

She took another look at the black and white photograph.

"Fancy Jim Foster being one of Bernie's closest friends."

Celia thought they were an unlikely pairing…

Poor Bernie had been murdered, one cold January night. He'd been waiting patiently at a pelican crossing – stabbed in the back by an unknown assailant – dead before he hit the ground.

As far as Celia knew, no-one had been charged with Bernie's murder. At the time, rumours were rife, he'd been 'bumped off' by a rival, someone he'd put out of business. It certainly made sense. Bernie's much-loved Princess Stores were the talk of the clothing trade. It was inevitable – his phenomenal success would create enemies as well as friends...

Two or three witnesses (waiting at the pelican crossing) suggested the young man hurrying away from the scene, wearing jeans and a grey hoodie, may have had something to do with the murder.

Hopefully, one day, the police would re-open the enquiry, it would be labelled (like so many others) a 'cold case'. Then and only then the murderer might be discovered...

How could anyone forget Bernie? He was irreplaceable. Almost every evening his chubby face had appeared on television screens; he was a real 'Cockney geezer' a self-made man.

Bernie's advertisements, planned and designed by The Foster Advertising Agency, always began in the same way – he'd look straight at the camera, give a wink and a cheeky smile, then say: "Hello, ladies!"

He'd go on and on about his Princess Stores (the generous gift of a free lipstick and nail-varnish) and remind the viewers that no matter what your age, they would find something special, just for you.

The Princess Stores were second to none: women loved their huge array of clothing, inexpensive but always top quality. He'd cornered the market where fashion was concerned, other retailers didn't stand a chance.

Bernie was so much more than a businessman; he was a philanthropist who gave away his millions, quietly, without fuss or need of praise...

It was because the public adored him that Bernie's murder was reported in such lurid detail by the tabloid press – becoming no less than a feeding frenzy...

No-one arranges a funeral better than the residents of the East End of London. It must be showy, brash, extravagant, whilst at the same time retaining an air of respect and grandeur.

Ronnie and Reggie Kray (infamous London gangsters throughout the 1950s and 60s) had been given a 'no expenses spared' send-off.

Many residents considered another high-profile funeral to be well overdue. A few unsympathetic souls, lacking in good taste, considered it to be something well worth looking forward to...

Bernie's funeral procession had been a sight to behold. A pair of black Hungarian horses (chosen for their even temperament) pulled the glass-windowed carriage. Both driver and groom looked immaculate in their traditional Victorian livery.

The carriage took a slow, respectful drive through the East End, stopping for a few moments outside Bernie's mum's council house in Whitechapel, the place where he'd spent his childhood.

Over three thousand people lined the streets to watch Bernie's cortege go by – many of the older generation were in tears…

Chapter 10

Complications

"Jim, I need to see you, it's very important. I'm just going to make some coffee so come over in ten minutes."

"Hang on Celia, I'm busy, I'm right in the middle of something…"

"You might well be, but if you don't come over, you'll live to regret it!"

The line went dead.

Jim was painting the highly decorative architrave surrounding the kitchen door; it had become damaged, possibly due to the delivery of a new washing machine and dishwasher. This original woodwork dated back to the late 18th century and stood the test of time. He could tell that at some point several coats of gloss had been burnt off and fresh primer and undercoat applied.

He'd filled the scrapes and scratches, rubbed it down and now with a fresh lick of white gloss it was looking good.

He stood in the hallway looking thoughtful. I'd better paint around the other downstairs doors too, they're all looking rather dingy…

He nodded his head and sighed.

"Yes, once I've finished tidying the garden and pruning the roses, still, there's no rush."

He took the paintbrush into the garage, leaving it upright in a jar of white spirit.

Why do people always ring at a bad time? Celia Bamford, what could she possibly want? I didn't appreciate her tone either, fancy speaking to me like that.

Celia was about to see a very different side of Jim. No smile when she opened the front door, just a sigh of impatience. She noticed some white paint on his checky shirt and smiled to herself, I bet that's a first!

She sensed Jim was in a bad mood. She smirked; he'll be even more upset when he hears what I have to say...

"I don't wish to be rude, Celia, but as you can see, I'm busy painting."

"Come through to the kitchen – the coffee is ready. Would you care for a slice of fruit cake, still lovely and warm?"

Why not, thought Jim, I may as well get something out of this bizarre visit.

Jim was grateful for small mercies: at least she didn't beg him to sit next to her, on the sofa. He felt relaxed. Having the kitchen table between them gave him a sense of security. It performed the role of a shield: the large, solid table leg prevented Celia's wandering hands from stroking his thighs or indeed, any other part of his anatomy!

Jim adored women: he flirted outrageously but only on his terms. The ladies in question must be (in his eyes) desirable or at least, good fun: in other words, nothing like Celia...

Jim glanced at his watch then began drumming his fingers on the table. Celia took the hint.

"Okay Jim, now you've enjoyed coffee and cake, I've something to tell you, or perhaps I should say – something to ask you."

Jim sighed. He wasn't in the mood for playing games.

"Well, go on, spit it out."

"I believe your beloved wife died in *Oxford,* is that correct? Just months before your planned move to Eastbourne?"

"Yes, you know she did, what the hell is this? Some sort of inquisition?"

"No Jim – it's about telling the truth. Your wife died in *Eastbourne,* St Christopher's House, an up-market residential nursing home. I've just been looking at it on Google Earth…

She stared at him, her mouth tight and her lips pursed.

"I read her obituary in the archives of the Eastbourne Herald. Please don't deny it, I'm nobody's fool. Why did you lie? What are you afraid of? What are you hiding?"

Jim could feel the blood draining from his face, he hoped Celia hadn't noticed. He'd become adept at telling lies, however this time he'd been unprepared. Her questions were snappy, full of confidence and right out of the blue...

He smiled, weakly.

"How about another mug of coffee? I need some caffeine first, then I'll tell you all about it.

Celia refilled his mug then pushed the sugar bowl towards him. His mood had softened, he was looking melancholy...

"I'll try not to become emotional. Molly was the love of my life: a proud lady, always thinking of others. She had a tendency to support lost causes, the smaller, less well-known charities, especially those caring for wild animals. Foxes, yes, she loved foxes."

111

Jim nodded his head then sighed, as if at any moment he might be reduced to tears...

"Molly was well known in the Oxford area for her charity work, which, unsurprisingly, gave her a high profile. She appeared frequently on local television and managed to help raise a great deal of money for our local hospice...

"After her devastating stroke, I whisked her away from the public eye, it's what she would have wanted. She would have hated the thought of people visiting her or pitying her. She'd become a pathetic creature robbed of all dignity.

"After Molly died, peacefully in her sleep, I had a nervous breakdown, I hardly knew night from day. I didn't think I could live without her...

"I had no idea – until you told me – that Mr Simms, the manager, had taken it upon himself to mention her death in the local newspaper. I do wish he'd asked me first."

Jim stood up, he looked angry. Why was he here, being questioned like this? It was ridiculous. He could tolerate no more of this ghastly woman, her inappropriate behaviour or her nosiness. He walked towards the front door.

"Come back here, Jim Foster, I haven't finished with you yet!"

"Haven't you, Celia? Well, that's tough. Leave me alone – I don't wish to be your friend or heaven forbid, your lover. For God's sake, woman, get that into your silly little head."

Celia smiled in a rather self-satisfied way. She'd saved the best 'til last. She raised her voice though Jim was no more than three metres away.

"Tell me, Jim, does the name Georgia de Vere mean anything to you?"

Jim counted to ten. He could visualize putting his hands around her neck and squeezing until he'd choked the life out of her; he'd be doing the world a favour...

Celia narrowed her eyes. He'd been shocked when she stroked his thigh, he should have been over the moon! How dare he spurn her advances; this was pay-back time. She took a deep breath then carried on.

"Breaking and entering, wasn't it? Oh dear, not what I'd expect from a man who'd had the world at his feet.

"The Fortune Teller's Handbook, yes, that was its name. Call yourself a man? Terrified of a Victorian book that's falling to pieces? Oh, dear, what a wimp. Poor little Jimmy Foster!"

Celia started to laugh – throwing back her head – she was hysterical. This was her moment, she felt euphoric. She looked across at Jim, nothing but hatred and loathing loomed large in his eyes.

Her tone changed to one of pure sarcasm…

"Anyway, dearest Jim, who was this whore, this woman with a fancy name? Georgia de Vere – huh, your mistress, I suppose…

"You left poor Molly to rot in a nursing home, you bastard. Was she aware you were making love to another woman?"

Jim could take no more of her insults. He rushed across the room his anger set free. He grabbed Celia by the shoulders, shaking her violently, making her head swing back and forth at an alarming rate. He slapped her across the face, leaving a red mark.

"Shut up, woman! Don't you dare mention my late wife's name. You didn't know her – you're not fit to walk in her shadow…"

He let go of her – he had to otherwise he would have killed her. Celia had been spying on him, trawling the internet, looking for dirt; why would she do such a thing? Anything would do, as long as it embarrassed him or caused him pain.

What was the saying? *Hell, hath no fury, like a woman scorned.*

Instead of being terrified, Celia appeared to be turned-on by his violent outburst. Her beady eyes looked bigger than usual – the pupils dilated by such a passionate, anger-filled confrontation…

"No need to worry, I promise not to tell anyone about your dodgy past or even suggest you considered killing me. Admit it, you wanted to put your hands around my neck and choke me! Look, all you have to do is be nice to me, love me, you know what I mean, don't you?

"Come on, Jim, you're tempted to make love to me, right now, aren't you? While you're still angry and your heart is racing? I won't complain if you get rough with me, you can do anything you want, I mean it – *anything!*

"Let's share a glass of whisky, we'll take it up to my bedroom and see what happens; quick, before the moment passes…"

"Don't be ridiculous, woman, you must know by now, I don't fancy you!"

"Yes, okay, I'm aware of that. However, I've got a vivid imagination – I can pretend you love me – if you'll just give me a chance."

Celia put her arms around Jim's waist, pulling him towards her, pressing herself against him. She tried to kiss him but he turned his head away.

"Be careful. You need to think things through, your options are limited. I don't imagine the lovely Olivia would want to sleep with a man who has a criminal record, do you?

"Naturally, it's my duty to put her in the picture. Unless, of course, you can persuade me to change my mind."

Celia started to cry – quietly at first – then the sobbing began, she was gasping for breath. Jim was embarrassed by her behaviour.

"There's no point in turning on the waterworks. I shall finish my drink then I'm going home. You can tell Olivia what you damn well like. You can tell the whole bloody village.

"Anyway, who said I fancy Olivia?"

Alan had been gentle, meek and mild, he hated any form of nastiness or confrontation, he crumbled under pressure.

Jim Foster was made of sterner stuff he was a seasoned businessman. Celia was small fry, he'd taken on the big boys and won…

When Jim left, without another word, Celia didn't move a muscle until she heard the front door close.

She'd made a complete fool of herself. This afternoon's performance was best forgotten. It was between her and Jim, it was something private, never to be mentioned again. Celia wiped away her tears and blew her nose; she knew when she was beaten.

Chapter 11

Worrying Thoughts

Jim sat in his favourite armchair a glass of whisky within reach. He sighed, why does life have to be so complicated?

At least his garden was looking lovely; a little jaded but still plenty of autumn colour. Mother Nature rarely let you down…

Every spring, as if by magic, thousands of bulbs pushed their way through the cold, damp soil. Each new purchaser of Gallica Rose had received the same unexpected treat: a carpet of dazzling colours.

Purple and white crocuses followed by cyclamens (pink and magenta) all surrounded by drifts of pure white snowdrops. Many were growing snugly against clumps of primroses and all of them hiding away beneath ancient trees – taking cover from damaging frosts. Some of the bulbs had been planted way back in the 1950s but continued to multiply and spread.

This particular morning, Jim enjoyed his breakfast: fresh coffee and two slices of buttered toast, spread generously with thick marmalade. It made a pleasant change from cereals.

Perhaps putting Celia in her place had improved his appetite. He'd tried not to be too unkind but her behaviour was weird in the extreme. Whatever possessed her to trawl the internet, scouring local and national newspapers, desperate for gossip? He was amazed she'd found anything. The poor woman was deranged...

Jim frowned, I hope to God she didn't discover a connection between me and Bernie P Epstein. Highly unlikely. Anyway, as everyone knew at the time of Bernie's murder, we were very good pals. My company was responsible for every one of the Princess Store's highly successful adverts. Yes, indirectly I was the man who helped Bernie become a millionaire!

Even Celia was unable to discover Jim's darkest secrets – the things that kept him awake at night, gave him indigestion and gnawed at his stomach.

Suddenly, the goldfinches appeared, he counted nine. Such noisy little devils. He must remember to buy some more sunflower hearts. Perhaps he'd order some online, a larger bag this time, free delivery and much cheaper too.

Every morning, after breakfast, Jim re-filled both containers, he was amazed by the amount these little birds could eat. He was convinced they were sitting there, hiding in the trees, watching, waiting for him to appear.

Suddenly, a sparrowhawk flew down, its talons grabbing hold of an unsuspecting blackbird. Within seconds the hawk returned to the huge cherry tree, its prey just another tasty meal. Jim felt guilty – if he hadn't thrown a slice of burnt toast onto the lawn perhaps the blackbird wouldn't have been there. He couldn't bear to see the suffering of any wild animal.

The nights were beginning to draw in, it used to make him feel melancholy, but not this year. The yellow, red and orange leaves (falling softly onto the lawn) failed to lower his spirits.

The moment he'd walked into the kitchen, wearing his towelling dressing gown, an urge to turn on the central heating prevailed. Thirty minutes, first thing, made all the difference...

The Michaelmas daisies were coming into flower and the dahlias looked as if they'd been in situ for years, flowers the size of saucers, unspoilt by damaging winds. Burgundy and white flowers, Jim's favourite combination.

There was much to be done but exercise was good for him – a healthy form of distraction, preventing him from worrying about the past. An hour each day was his intention.

The lawn was rectangular: it had been described (on the estate agent's blurb) as being 'a generous size and well-maintained.'

Jim fancied a ride-on mower – he'd always wanted one. Well, why not? It might be fun. He could make straight lines, back and forth, then amuse himself by creating neat circles around each of the fruit trees. It would be effortless, saving energy for the boring things like weeding and pruning, jobs which seemed never-ending.

Whilst showing him the rear garden of Gallica Rose, the estate agent, Lenny Barnes, directed Jim towards several gnarled old trees, their twisted branches covered with lichen.

"See them trees, Mr Foster? I've heard tell they produce masses of fruit, mainly Victoria plums and Bramley cooking apples. The trees were planted way back in the 1930s – by that posh bloke – Colonel something or other...

"Years ago, the local kids used to climb over that back wall, scrumping, then go home with belly-ache not realising them Bramleys was only for cooking! Yeah, their mums gave 'em a clip round the ear – they'd been told to nick the apples and take 'em home for a pie – not scoff 'em! In them days, young kids were ever so good at scrumping, poaching too!"

Jim had to laughed. Lenny Barnes was a lively character, great fun, he enjoyed being with him. Another cheeky Cockney – just like Bernie P Epstein…

A vast quantity of fresh fruit would be of little interest to Jim, but he wouldn't be surprised in the least if some of the local ladies (who enjoyed making jam, pies or crumbles) decided to befriend him, just as the fruit was ripening!

Whilst living in Eastbourne, Jim treated himself to three huge terracotta pots, it had taken hours to fill them with bulbs.

The removal men had looked annoyed when he pointed to the pots (still filled to the top with compost and bulbs) and insisted, they must go inside the removal van. However, with three strong men and a sack-barrow, they'd managed with ease.

They'd smile appreciatively though, when Jim opened his wallet and handed each man a crisp twenty-pound note, but he didn't stop there, he must be remembered as a fantastic bloke, generous, charismatic...

"Oh, I nearly forgot – these are for you. Many thanks, lads, you've done a splendid job. No breakages..."

Jim smiled warmly as he handed over three bottles of top-quality Merlot.

When the empty removal van left Bridgeford (on its way back to Eastbourne) it carried three happy workers who would go home and tell their wives about Jim Foster. They'd probably go on and on – all evening. Yeah, what a great bloke, twenty quid and a bottle of red wine! If only all their customers were like him.

Jim had been happy in Eastbourne, there was always something going on. The sea air blew away the cobwebs and made him feel alive...

What a shame Georgia had been so cruel, so unforgiving. They'd been crazy about each other – she'd never find another man like him!

Once details of his crime had been displayed in the Eastbourne Gazette (allowing the whole county to read about him and smirk) he had no choice but to leave. Jim was a man who loved attention, revelled in it, but he could do without this sort of notoriety.

What if his neighbours were talking about him, even worse, laughing at him!

"There he goes," they'd say, *"can you believe it? Fancy breaking into Mrs de Vere's bungalow! He should be ashamed of himself. It's not as if he needs the money. Someone told me he was a millionaire!"*

In Jim's eyes he'd done nothing wrong: it was only breaking and entering. Georgia's house and contents insurance were up-to-date – just a lot of fuss about nothing...

Besides, it wasn't his fault – it was all down to that wretched book – how he loathed it! When the little book was consulted, Georgia and her enthusiastic friends were given encouraging news, time after time:

'An inheritance will be coming your way. A rewarding trip to foreign shores. Excellent health.

Wealth and success through hard work. An unexpected marriage proposal.'

The list of possible opportunities and experiences went on and on until Jim felt like screaming. However, when *he* selected a playing card and looked inside the book to decipher its meaning, the book handed out nothing but dire warnings:

'Beware the elderly gentleman, he is obstinate and hot tempered. Your lover is surrounded by death. A scheming, devious liar. A man not to be trusted. You will never marry your sweetheart.'

Now, when he thought of Georgia, he felt angry and let-down.

After the break-in she should have tried to see things from his point of view, not laughed (along with her friends) when the evil little book dealt out yet another spiteful warning. Georgia should have thrown it in the bin or better still, burnt it – not gone running to the Sussex Constabulary!

It was always the same: nothing was ever Jim's fault, it was other people, they made him do bad things...

Chapter 12

Fun and Games

Jim enjoyed keeping fit. He'd always been proud of his physique, so much so that he was unable to walk past a full-length mirror without admiring himself. He must stay positive. One day soon a delightful lady would enter his life, fall madly in love with him and all would be well. Of one thing he was certain, the lucky lady would be nothing, absolutely nothing, like Celia Bamford!

Jim decided not to reveal his true age. Why complicate things? If people assumed he was sixty (thus deducting seven years) well, so what? In his eyes, he looked so good, age became irrelevant. He chuckled to himself...

"A babe magnet, what a ridiculous expression, still, it suits me. I've been irresistible to the fairer sex since the age of sixteen."

Jim had fond memories of a certain Geography teacher, twenty-four-year-old Sandra Weeks; she was the only female teacher at his popular, but hugely expensive, public school...

One day she'd asked Jim to stay behind after school, she needed help setting up a new project. Had she been aware he'd celebrated his sixteenth birthday – only the previous week? Jim smiled happily as he recalled the events of that memorable afternoon. The petite red-head, Miss Weeks, had practically dragged him into the stock room, saying she needed help lifting 'something heavy.' She'd pulled off his tie then unbuttoned his shirt in a rather frantic manner.

Yes, he'd learned a lot that afternoon – although none of it would be found on the school's curriculum...

Jim shook his head. My goodness, if that happened today, Miss Weeks would end up in prison and rightly so!

Jim considered dying his hair, not jet black as favoured by some men, no, more of a golden brown.

A stark vision of the late Ronnie Regan, actor and former President of the United States, came readily to mind. Such a likeable chap, but his hair (so obviously dyed) had been the colour of beetroot. He smirked, best leave well along. Grey hair used to be called distinguished, what a nice word...

Jim cheered up when his thoughts turned to Shelly, the vivacious hair stylist. He'd fancied her the moment he set eyes on her. He was convinced she'd been flirting with him, after all, she had squeezed his shoulder when she'd offered him a mug of coffee. However, she might think he was too old...

He frowned. There could be twenty years between us, although far less if I lie about my age. He was in with a chance. Shelly was divorced and she wasn't seeing anyone, her brother happened to mention it whilst snipping away at Jim's thick, wavy hair.

Perhaps she'd see him as a 'Sugar-daddy' a man who would buy her nice things and take her to expensive places: five-star hotels and Michelin starred restaurants then whisk her away for an exotic holiday or a week-end in Paris. Jim loved making grand gestures.

He certainly knew how to please the ladies. He had the money and the necessary *'je ne sais quoi'*.

Jim had yet to walk through the door of Temptations, although this was the second-time he'd admired their window display. The twins were watching him, discretely, pretending to gaze out of the shop window. He looked at one of them and smiled, even giving a little wave. Alice giggled, blushed then turned away. Perhaps he should ignore them, encouraging them might be a mistake…

The steak and ale pies looked delicious, perhaps he'd buy one for his tea.

"Good morning, Jim," said a friendly, female voice.

He looked over his shoulder, his face lighting up when he saw who it was.

"Hello, Shelly, I've been thinking about you."

"*Oh, have you now!*" she replied, looking at him in a way that made his heart race.

"I can recommend those apple turnovers, they're delicious, thin buttery pastry and loads of filling."

"Slight problem, Shelly – my garden is littered with fallen apples so it would be rather pointless buying anything like that."

She laughed, "Oh, I see. Well, you'd better stick to the steak and ale pies then."

"Shelly, you are more than welcome to have some apples, that is, if you enjoy cooking. I don't mean windfalls either – you can select your own – nature's finest, straight off the tree!"

He smiled, boyishly, in the way that made him irresistible to women.

"Really? Thanks, Jim. Shall I pop round this afternoon, after three?"

It was a Monday so the salon was closed, she'd been wondering what to do with herself. Ironing, or Jim Foster? No contest. Should she take Jet with her? Why not? He was a good boy and Jim was so sweet, he must be an animal lover. Jim and Jet, she smiled, even their names were compatible...

Shelly was eager to see Jim's beautiful home. She knew the Evesham Road well – long and winding – but she'd taken no notice of Gallica Rose.

She telephoned her mum who was most surprised to hear where her daughter was going...

"Oh, you lucky girl, I'd love to look round that place. Gallica Rose is special, you'd never find a better example of an 18th century thatched cottage. Someone told me it's been photographed for biscuit tins, souvenirs, that sort of thing. It must have cost him a fortune. I shall expect you to pop round and tell me all about it."

After a cup of tea and a tour round Jim's immaculate garden, Shelly had an idea.

"Look, I'm in no rush and Jet's happy nosing around in the garden, so, would you like me to make you an apple pie? I love cooking. Assuming you've got all the ingredients. Do you have flour?"

"Yes, I've certainly got a bag of flour. I made toad in the hole, yesterday, bit of a disaster, the batter failed to rise, too thin I expect. Oh, I think there's a rolling pin, somewhere."

The cooked apple pie smelt very tempting. Since Molly's stroke and her subsequent death, he'd missed the smell of home cooking.

Jim inhaled, deeply: the aroma filled the kitchen, it was comforting. Someone had cared enough to create something special – just for him. Shelly squeezed Jim's hand.

"Come on then, let's cut the pie while it's still warm. I'd love a slice before I go…"

Jim tutted, there was no cream in the fridge so they made do with vanilla ice-cream. They sat together in front of the wood-burning stove. There was a comfortable silence between them, neither feeling the need to make small-talk. Shelly stretched then kicked off her black patent-leather stiletto heels…

The heat from the fire was intense. Within minutes she'd removed her thick jumper, revealing a pale blue V neck T shirt. Jim, always the gentleman, looked away, gazing firmly into the flickering flames…

"How about a glass of wine?"

"I can't, honestly, I should be going home. Jet must be hungry by now – he's been running around in your garden for ages. He loves it!"

Jim had a bright idea.

"I wonder – would he fancy a couple of pork sausages? There's two, already cooked, left over from yesterday's disastrous meal."

Shelly laughed and gave him a hug.

"Oh, bless, I'll have to give you some cooking lessons. Yes, I'm sure Jet would enjoy your leftovers!"

They walked back to the sofa holding a large glass of Riesling. Jet yawned and snuggled up beside her feet. He had no problem with Jim's cooking! Another couple of logs were thrown onto the blazing fire: the sap began to spit – Jet jumped and moved away. Shelly looked at Jim then sighed.

"Thanks, Jim, I've had a lovely relaxing afternoon. I really ought to go home now but the wine's made me feel so sleepy, I can't be bothered."

Jim lifted her chin with an index finger and looked into her big green eyes.

"Well, *darling,* who says you have too?"

Gotcha! This was *his* moment and he knew it. He'd reeled her in, hook, line and sinker. All it took was one word – *darling...*

Jim's manly voice made women act foolishly, as if hypnotized by his charm.

His public-school accent may have sent shivers down Shelly's spine but deep-down he was a snob, a bastard, like most men born into a life of luxury and privilege...

Shelly sensed he was dangerous – a man you'd be wise not to upset – but wasn't that part of the attraction?

Jim neither knew nor cared a jot about political correctness. He adored women and they adored him. Shelly giggled and gave him another hug. He kissed her, gently but longingly. She stared at him, surprised but not offended. She wanted him to make love to her but felt confused by the strength of her own feelings. Who was this man, this handsome stranger? She hardly knew him.

"Jim, what's happening to us? This is all so sudden, I thought we were just good friends…"

Jim was quiet for a few moments.

"Look, neither of us is in a relationship so we can do whatever we please. Don't fight it…"

"Feel free to go upstairs and have a lie down, I won't follow you – I'll stay outside with Jet. There are two newly decorated bedrooms and a box room. Try the room over-looking the garden, the one with the

William Morris wallpaper, it's got a very large double bed."

She laughed, flirtatiously. Jim was so cute. She stood up, swayed slightly, then walked towards him holding out her hand.

"But Jimbo, I might get lost – it's such a big cottage. I'd feel like Goldilocks, trying out all the beds. You haven't got three bears upstairs, have you?"

"No, I can honestly say, there are no bears upstairs."

Jim chuckled, were his dreams about to come true? They'd both had a little too much wine, anything could happen.

"What if I strayed into your bedroom by mistake? That would never do. You'd better come upstairs with me. Oh, don't forget to bring another bottle of that lovely Riesling!"

Jim smiled, perhaps Mateo Verde had been right after all, he should have ordered that whirlpool bath! He'd certainly like to see Shelly trying it out…

Chapter 13

Lenny...

Lenny Barnes was not a man you'd want to upset. His lack of control and short temper were something to behold...

In the mid-eighties, Ernie Barnes decided to move his family away from the East End – it wasn't good for the boy – he was getting in with the wrong crowd. With one son in prison (a five-year stretch) Ernie was determined, young Lenny would not be joining him.

After a favourable phone call (during a rather lacklustre weekend) an excitable Lenny had grabbed the keys to Gallica Rose. He'd looked at his partner, then grinned mischievously.

"Steve, I'm off to meet a Mr James Foster, sounds like a right toff. Wish me luck, matey, this could the big one!"

Steve shook his head. Ernie Barnes had been a good salesman but his son was a day-dreamer and far too excitable. The word liability sprung readily to mind.

Jim Foster parked in the gravel driveway of Gallica Rose. A man like Jim, who demanded punctuality, should always set an example – he was eight minutes early…

On Lenny's arrival he folded his copy of the Daily Telegraph, put it on the passenger seat then climbed out of the car.

"Cor, nice one," whispered Lenny, looking enviously at Jim's top of the range BMW. Even better, the man had style, yeah, a cherished number-plate and a bloody expensive one too! He liked punters with good taste and plenty of money.

Lenny was impressed by but at the same time slightly in awe of this 'old school' English gentleman. Jim Foster – what a classy geezer, good looking too. Must be over sixty. I bet he's bedded more women than I've had hot dinners. Wish I had some of that public-school charm. It ain't right though, gives a bloke an unfair advantage.

Lenny's thoughts gathered apace.

If Mr Foster is hoping to buy Gallica Rose he must be loaded – not only that – he said it would be a cash purchase. Cash? You're having a laugh. It's one and a quarter million quid! Blimey, there'll be a tidy bit of commission coming my way.

Lenny's summing-up of Jim's personality was not only accurate, it was hardly surprising. Jim charmed everyone he met, male or female.

The moment they entered the cottage Lenny knew he was onto a winner; he'd need no powers of persuasion with this property. Positive vibes, call it what you will, Mr Foster had fallen in love with the place.

Once they'd sauntered round the garden (Lenny pointing out a few interesting facts) Mr Foster had a certain glint in his eye and Lenny had his sale: this was his lucky day…

"Yes, Lenny, I'll take it. I'd like to move in as soon as possible. Any problems I should know about?"

Two weeks after Jim's arrival he'd popped in to see Lenny and ended up staying for a mug of instant coffee, a chocolate digestive and a chat.

Lenny was feeling out of sorts, Steve Hornet was on holiday, two weeks in Portugal, lucky devil. He was cheesed off – the market was painfully quiet – he could do with some company. He liked Jim, easy to talk to and a good listener, empathetic too.

Lenny's recent divorce had dragged him down and now, to top it all, his mum, Lily, had dropped a bombshell.

She was moving back to the Smoke. He certainly hadn't seen that coming...

Since the death of his father, she'd been lonely, unsettled. With six grandchildren, all living in Bethnal Green, it was no surprise. Lily longed to return to London, she missed her family. She didn't drive either which made life difficult.

"Sorry, Len, I'm going, I've made up me mind. You can carry on with the business and stay in the house, yer dad always wanted it that way. I'll be okay living with Debs, she's got five bedrooms, plenty of room, we won't get on each other's nerves."

Debbie (her first child) had done well for herself she'd married a solicitor then given up her job in order to care for their young daughters.

Now, after moving to Orpington, they were living the good life. A desirable area, big garden and just a short train journey from the East End and her boisterous family…

Since Lenny and Shelly's divorce, he'd been bad-tempered and difficult to live with. Lily sighed, maybe her son was better off on his own. No more arguments or heated rows…

Lily felt a great sense of relief, only one week to go. She'd be happier back in London, well away from her troublesome son. The Cotswolds might be a beautiful area, low crime rate too, but she'd rather be back with her own kind.

Lenny was driving along Fosdyke Way when he spotted them – Shelly and Jim – walking through the park, hand in hand. They looked good together, relaxed, as if they hadn't a care in the world. Lenny was furious, he couldn't believe his eyes.

As there was a cold north-easterly wind, they'd both grabbed a scarf before venturing outside. Jim had ordered the matching scarves (cream and beige stripes) from John Lewis, just the previous week. Shelly adored Jim's surprise present, pure cashmere, it made her feel special. Was she more than a little besotted with him?

"Just look at 'em," whispered Lenny, "they're wearing matching scarves, how pathetic is that? It makes you wanna puke."

How he wished his binoculars were still inside the glove compartment…

Jim stopped briefly beneath a large horse chestnut tree, picked up something (presumably a conker) and handed it to Shelly. She laughed, then bent down to pick up a few more.

What the hell is he doing with my missus?

Lenny signalled right, turned into Gloucester Avenue, then made a three-point turn at the end of the road. Now that he was facing Fosdyke Park he could watch them as they strolled by. Lenny glanced in the rear-view mirror, his cheeks looked pale and blotchy.

The 'loving couple' were holding hands no more. Jim's arm was around her waist, he pulled her towards him then kissed her, lightly, on the lips. Even from a distance he could tell, by her body language, Shelly was relaxed and enjoying every single moment spent with her new lover...

Oh, how cosy they looked!

He's a fast worker. Oh yeah, of course, he's been in the salon, had his hair cut. She's forty-seven so he must be at least thirteen years older. He's punching above his weight. Yeah, flippin' smoothie. Who was Lenny trying to kid? With Jim's money, good looks and charisma, Shelly couldn't resist him – who could blame her?

That evening, after enjoying cod and chips, Lenny Barnes turned on his lap-top. Lily snoozed in front of the six o'clock news.

James Foster was typed into the search bar: he might be lucky and find something interesting or better still – incriminating. Jim might be a con-man, he might be a bank robber. Lenny laughed, umm, highly unlikely. He trawled the internet searching every site he thought capable of throwing up a little scandal. He came across an excellent photograph of Jim and Bernie P Epstein – quite an old one though. He could remember the name, yes, he'd owned a chain of shops, the Princess Stores. His mum would remember them but he wouldn't disturb her – he'd ask her later…

"Goodness me, Len, Bernie P Epstein, that's a blast from the past."

Lily Barnes seemed surprised by her son's probing questions.

"Well, I can tell you lots about poor old Bernie, although I never 'eard of no Jim Foster, not back in

147

them days. Bernie was murdered, all the papers was full of it. I cried – honest I did…

"Proper East End boy, yeah, that's why I remember him so clearly. Jewish, of course. Everybody loved him, generous but modest with it. They say he gave away half his fortune.

"He was murdered on January 27th Holocaust Memorial Day. I bet it was one of them hateful right-wing groups, you know, them bloody Nazi types.

"Bernie was stabbed in the back as he waited at a pelican crossing. He'd been on his way to Whitechapel to visit his old mum. He'd got flowers and chocolates for her, yeah, they was squashed flat in the rush to 'elp him.

"The police and newspapers claimed he was murdered by a rival – someone he'd put out of business, who knows…

"I'll tell you something, son, there'll never be another Bernie. Do you know, within a year his business empire went bust? Umm, bankrupt, it was as if them stores had never existed."

Lily walked into the kitchen and turned on the kettle, she shook her head and wiped away a few tears. She was thinking of Miriam Epstein, Bernie's mum, sitting in front of the television cameras, begging for information; it had been painful to watch. Lily sighed.

"What a wicked old world."

Chapter 14

Blackmail

"Is that you, Jim? It's Lenny Barnes. You and me need to have a few words..."

Jim was surprised by two things: Lenny's lack of basic good manners (he'd always called him Mr Foster, never Jim) and even more so, by his aggressive tone.

"Oh, it's you – hello Lenny. Well, I hope it's important, I'm picking someone up in ten minutes. We're going to the cinema – the Plaza in Chipping Norton – we don't want to be late."

To say Lenny's reply was sarcastic would have been an understatement.

"Oh, the cinema, is it? How cosy. Don't forget your popcorn. I assume you're taking Shelly, my ex-missus? Well, I'm not happy Jim, not happy at all. We might be divorced but I don't appreciate the likes of you muscling in..."

"Fed up with playing conkers in Fosdyke Park, are we? Yeah, I saw the pair of you, it was embarrassing. She'll soon give you the elbow."

Jim caught his breath, surely not, Shelly, married to Lenny? He was losing his touch, he'd failed to make the connection – Barnes, yes, of course! Fancy being married to that spiv! Who the hell did he think he was?

No wonder she didn't talk about her ex-husband – well, other than to say he was an idiot and nasty when drunk. He'd discovered an ugly side to Lenny, he'd better nip it in the bud.

"Being as you're divorced you have little or no say in the matter. Shelly can do whatever she wants – the clue is in the word ex, she's your ex-wife. Do us all a favour, Lenny, grow up and don't you dare ring me again!"

Jim slammed down the receiver…

During Jim's speedy, hassle-free purchase of Gallica Rose, it'd been necessary for Lenny to deal with one of the negotiators working for Stuart Marquis and Partners, the agency handling the sale of Jim's bungalow.

The bungalow in Eastbourne had been purchased by the first couple who'd viewed it, hardly surprising, it was immaculate. Even so – there were phone calls, solicitors' letters, the signing and exchanging of contracts, plus negotiating a satisfactory moving date.

Lenny thought the staff were an odd bunch, apart from young Dennis Smithers. He wondered why the rest of them seemed so snooty, there was nothing special about Eastbourne – just a load of retired people with plenty of cash and too much time on their hands. Dennis was okay, you could have a chat and a laugh with him, in fact a rather warm friendship had developed.

"Hi, Dennis, it's me, Lenny Barnes, Bridgeford. How are you doing, mate?"

Dennis Smithers happened to be in the office on his own, he was bored so a call from Lenny was most welcome. He laughed, loudly.

"Cor, well I never, Lenny Barnes. You old rogue, I thought I'd heard the last of you!"

"No, you can't get rid of me that easily! Now then, Dennis, I'm curious about Mr Smooth, you know, Jim Foster, Gallica Rose. What do you know about him? Any scandal? Seems like a good bloke, on the surface. I'm asking for a friend…"

"Yeah, course you are, mate," replied Dennis, giving a little chuckle…

"Funny you should ask about Mr Foster. Not long before he put his bungalow on the market, he had some sort of breakdown.

"He was seeing this woman, Georgia something (can't recall her surname) anyway, he broke into her place and nicked stuff, left it in a terrible mess. Not sure why, he doesn't seem like a weirdo. Anyway, he had to do community service, I read all about in the local paper. Take a look at the Eastbourne Herald, the archives, it must be there, there's stuff going back years. Dare I ask why 'your friend' wants to know?"

Lenny smiled to himself.

"Well, Dennis, my old friend, let's just say, he's got his grubby paws on something that don't belong to him."

"Oh, damn, sorry Len, the boss is outside, parking his car, he's in a foul mood today – I'll have to go. Pop in, mate, if you're down this way. Cheers then, bye."

The line went dead. That was interesting, thought Lenny, good job I rang him. Sounds unlikely though – I hope he's got the right James Foster! He sniggered. I can't imagine Jim taking kindly to community service or wearing a high-viz jacket! He's a man who wouldn't want to get his hands dirty…

He checked the archives of the Eastbourne Herald (just as Celia had done before him) and found them most enlightening. Jim Foster, 'Mr Smooth', breaking and entering. Whatever next?

It was one-thirty when the phone rang. Jim grabbed it, his heart racing. When the phone rang, in the wee small hours, it was usually bad news…

"Yes, who is it?" he asked, his voice full of trepidation.

"Easy, mate, no need to panic."

Jim recognised Lenny's voice straight away, the Cockney accent and the once likeable, 'cheeky chappie' attitude. Jim winced, it's one-thirty in the morning and he calls me, mate!

"I assume you're on your own, Jim? The thing is, if my ex-wife was in your bed, right now, I wouldn't like it, no, not one little bit, in fact, I could get very nasty. I'd be obliged to come round there and sort you out.

"However, I'm not usually a violent man. It's your lucky day, Jimbo. Let's be civilized, shall we?"

Lenny stopped talking – eventually.

"What is it you're after, Lenny? Money, I suppose? Well, you've wasted your time. If you contact me again, I'll telephone the police."

"Yeah, you do that, chummy. One word to the police and I'll tell Shelly all about your shady past.

155

Breaking and entering, theft, too! Oh, dear, I don't think she'd like that, she's as honest as the day is long.

"Of course, it wouldn't only be Shelly I was telling, oh no, I can be quite loud when I want to, especially when I'm in Temptations…

"Poor old Jim – all them middle-aged ladies, lusting after your body. After I'd told them about your criminal record, well, let's face it – you'd never be able to show your face in there again…"

Lenny hadn't enjoyed himself so much for ages.

Jim sat down on the edge of the mattress. First Celia, now Lenny. What was the matter with these people, had they nothing better to do than search the internet for idle gossip?

"How much?" he asked, as he searched the bedside cabinet for painkillers. A tired-looking foil strip, containing two aspirins, was all he could find.

"That's better, Jim, you know it makes sense. Why don't we start with a nice round ten thousand pounds? I'm not greedy. By the way, if I see you with my ex-missus again, next time, it'll be twenty thousand pounds – do I make myself clear?

"You can afford it, so let's not mess about, eh? I'll tell you when and where, no rush…"

Lenny turned off his mobile.

He enjoyed threatening people, it made him feel powerful. He finished his can of extra-strong lager, turned off the bedside light and within minutes he was fast asleep.

Chapter 15

Reflections

After placing a mug of hot chocolate on the bedside cabinet, Jim climbed back into bed. He always kept a note pad and pencil handy; it was surprising how many bright ideas popped into his head when he should be fast asleep…

Fortunately, during Jim's recent visit to the office, Lenny had, unwittingly, answered many of Jim's queries…

Lenny: lives alone. Works at Barnes and Hornet. Mum has returned to London. Girlfriend? No. Address: 2 Warwick Terrace, next to alleyway. Check for side-gate etc. Burglary gone wrong? Strangled? Maybe. Use scarf or similar item belonging to victim – less chance of leaving DNA.

Jim felt like a bear with a sore head: he had the beginnings of a tension headache, no doubt the aspirins would help. This unpleasantness with Lenny was the last thing he needed.

Getting away with murder was extremely difficult and that was an understatement, so much could go wrong. Besides, murder was something he'd put behind him. Was he becoming addicted? Surely not, after all, there must be easier alternatives.

"Still, I did get away with it, *twice!"*

Two murders, no connection whatsoever. According to the incompetent doctor who'd failed to do more than sign the death certificate, Molly's death was due to 'natural causes.' Jim chuckled, a smug smile upon his handsome face – he felt invincible – never a peep from the boys in blue...

At the height of his career, he'd enjoyed entertaining valued clients: for him, the cost was irrelevant. One of London's top casinos became a meeting place where Jim would flatter his clients and spoil them. The staff knew and respected him, he paid his bills, immediately and always left a generous tip.

"Put it on my tab," he'd say, as if money meant nothing to him.

Three course meals, fine wines, five-star accommodation and high-class prostitutes. Even their greed (in the form of gambling chips) was encouraged, nurtured, by the Foster Advertising Agency.

Whilst in the casino, Jim made a bee-line for a few well-known London villains. He bought drinks and flattered them as he absorbed their sordid tales of murder and robbery.

A 'friend of a friend' had (for a generous fee) planned, with much guile, the unforgivable and callous murder of Bernie P Epstein.

The whole thing went like a dream. Some eighteen-year-old drug addict (of low intellect, but well informed) followed his mentor's instructions calmly and methodically.

There may have been a few suspects, but no-one had ever been charged...

Jim had been very fond of Bernie. He'd been a trusted friend. What made Bernie decide to jump ship and sign an advertising contract with some 'know it all' American company? Jim's masterpiece would have been a runaway success, Bernie should have waited. Everything was in place, ready for the big 'reveal'. He'd been working on it, tirelessly, for over six months…

He'd been in line for a huge pay-out too, over one million pounds. Bernie had been an idiot, lured away by a lousy New York accent. Fancy working with Dale, Bloomberg and Cummings – cheaper, yes, but they lacked class. Their childish effort had a jazzy, corporate, feel. Wrong for the Princess Stores and wrong for the UK.

Bernie was a star in his own right, a Cockney geezer who deserved to be the front man in any new advertising campaign. Who decided to make a cartoon version of Bernie and give him a voice like Mickey Mouse? Oh dear – bad mistake!

Jim laughed, the ads were 'cringeworthy', to use one of his late father's favourite words. The Yanks simply didn't get it, they failed to understand Bernie's loveable personality. The adverts were a dismal failure, some might say an embarrassment.

Jim had been cast aside, he felt like a fool and his bank balance was suffering from the loss of Bernie's account. No-one did that to him and got away with it.

"Still, that's life," he whispered, shrugging his shoulders.

"If Bernie had stayed loyal to The Foster Advertising Agency, he'd still be alive today."

Empathy, guilt and forgiveness were missing from Jim's warped psyche.

Chapter 16

Perfect planning

Lenny's house displayed no visible burglar alarm, that was a good start. Jim planned to enter the property through a window, using the *modus operandi* he'd perfected when breaking into Georgia de Vere's bungalow. However, on that dark, stormy evening his confidence was sky-high. He knew she'd be out all evening, at the theatre, with her neighbour, Pauline.

From the moment he smashed the glass and squeezed through the bathroom window his heart was pounding like a drum. After searching Georgia's home for over and hour, he gave up. He was on a fool's errand – The Fortune Teller's Handbook was nowhere to be found. If the loathsome little book had been in its rightful place (in the sideboard drawer) the burglary would have been a thrilling and rewarding experience – one he would be more than happy to repeat!

Jim couldn't relax; suddenly, the whole idea of breaking into Lenny's house seemed a very bad move, far too risky.

His thoughts continued apace…

Breaking and entering could be described as a minor offence and even his lengthy community service was no punishment – being far more humiliating than distressing. However, planning to climb through a downstairs window in order to commit murder is in a very different league…

Jim had acquired information on Lenny's personal life although he knew very little about his friends. Did he go out with his mates, or to the local pub? If you break into someone's house with the sole intention of killing them, it's best to ensure they're at home and also, alone.

Jim nodded, feeling pleased with himself, he'd made the right decision. He'd had an about turn – a complete 360 degrees. Okay, if Lenny wants his ten thousand pounds, let him come and collect it. That's a far better option. Ply him with strong drink, catch him off guard, then strangle or suffocate him. There was no rush, he'd make a decision nearer the time…

Jim began muttering to himself, something he resorted to when under great pressure.

"Ah, but what if alcohol isn't enough? Lenny must be fifteen years younger than me, though not necessarily stronger or fitter! Even so, he'll put up one hell of a fight. Sleeping tablets or painkillers? Um, now there's a thought, although getting hold of them might be problematic. If I visit the surgery requesting a prescription for this type of medicine, the doctor (whom I've yet to meet) will see from my notes that I've never taken pills before, not for anything. I've always enjoyed excellent health. My visit will be remembered and not just for my charm and good looks, either."

Olivia, yes, of course! She's on strong painkillers, she mentioned them the other day.

Olivia had been happy to confide in Jim: she hated taking these wretched pills, they made her feel lethargic, but until she'd been given a new hip, she had no choice.

"If I didn't take them, I wouldn't be able to do anything and even worse, I'd get no sleep at all."

Jim was aware of Olivia's distress; he'd noticed dark circles appearing beneath her lovely eyes.

"Perfect," he whispered, "all I have to do now is get hold of the tablets!"

He sat in front of the patio doors, fascinated, nature at its finest. A female blackbird fought with a long, pinkish worm, stretching and pulling it; the blackbird was, unsurprisingly, the victor. New ideas and cunning plots flowed rapidly into his mind.

In the background he could hear a rotary mower, it could only be Charles, his neighbour. From the terrible racket he was making Charles was mowing the gravel too – no doubt stones were flying everywhere!

Charles was a retired accountant, a charming man with a once lively imagination and cheery disposition. Jim felt very sorry for him, there were obvious signs of Dementia…

166

Charles Greenwood's wife had died the previous year and maybe, because of his loss, his decline appeared to be gathering speed. The previous day when Jim hurried to the recycling bin with a pile of squashed cardboard boxes, Charles had smiled and waved at him.

"Oh, good evening, Jack!" he'd shouted, excitedly.

It was eight o'clock in the morning and Charles was wearing his pyjamas and dressing gown. He was bending down, weeding, blissfully unaware of the pouring rain. Jim rushed round immediately and persuaded Charles to go back inside. In an unusually caring mood, Jim stayed for a while, even making them both a mug of coffee.

However, he couldn't resist going on and on about Molly, how much he missed her and what a wonderful marriage they'd had.

Olivia tried to keep busy. Whenever the telephone rang, her heart missed a beat, was this the call she'd been waiting for? Had there been a cancellation? Perhaps, at last, she would be offered a date for her much-needed operation.

Olivia was able to mow the lawn as long as she stopped occasionally for a break. Jim had offered to help but she was a proud, independent lady.

"Thanks Jim, it's okay, I can manage. It's a powerful machine, all I have to do is point it in the right direction!"

They'd laughed about it – Jim admiring her cheerfulness and tenacity.

If I wait until Olivia is mowing the lawn (getting creative with a few nice stripes) I can nip through the hedge and straight into her kitchen. I bet she's got several boxes of painkillers – can't do without them – even if she keeps them upstairs, I'll have plenty of time to find them.

The following week, Jim carried out his devious plan. Olivia was determined to mow the lawn; heavy showers were forecast for the next few days so she must grit her teeth and get on with it.

Jim was relieved (and not for the first time) that Olivia's elderly pug, Boris, had been put to sleep. He'd insisted on driving her to the vets, she was very upset – she couldn't be expected to go alone...

Jim stood by the kitchen window, watching and waiting. When Olivia turned around, he would sneak through the small gap between the beech hedge and the garden shed and into her rear garden...

He checked over his shoulder, Olivia's back was towards him. He walked confidently through the unlocked backdoor and into her kitchen.

He looked down, irritated – just as he thought – he'd snagged several threads on his new burgundy jumper. A ragged hole appeared, below his elbow, the size of a twenty-pence coin.

"Oh, bugger that hedge. Never mind, I can afford another jumper, or another fifty, if I feel like it."

Jim looked out of Olivia's kitchen window and chuckled. There she goes, up and down, bless her, she's a lot tougher than she looks...

Now then, where are these pills?

Jim found some immediately, just where he thought they might be, in the small kitchen drawer beneath the kettle. Two packs, thirty tablets in each.

Oxycodone? Never heard of it, must be some new wonder drug. After opening the slim white box, he removed one foil strip (ten tablets) putting it straight into his shirt pocket. He was about to return the box to the kitchen drawer, then changed his mind. *No, I may as well take the lot, why not? As long as Olivia has another box, no reason why she should suffer…*

As he turned to leave, the doorbell rang, shrill, piercing, making him jump…

Jim took a deep breath, it was okay, the kitchen door was closed, he couldn't be seen from the hallway or the glass panel in the front door. He smiled. Olivia hadn't heard a thing due to the constant noise made by the motor-mower.

Before leaving the kitchen, Jim picked up a neatly folded but rather garish tea-towel: *'Welcome to*

Lyme Regis' was scrawled across the top and underneath was an image of the famous landmark, The Cobb. He shook his head, what an amateurish representation, a seven-year-old child could have done better.

He took a final look round then grabbed hold of a ripe pineapple, purchased by Olivia the previous day. He could smell its sweetness despite the thick, rough skin.

"Might come in handy," he whispered, with a knowing smile...

Once home, Jim examined the tablets: he was pleasantly surprised – not at all what he'd been expecting. The foil strips contained soft, bright-yellow, jelly-like capsules. All he had to do was snip off the end and save the liquid. The thought of grinding down a couple of hard white tablets had made him feel uneasy; they might remain gritty, even visible, at the bottom of a glass. He'd planned to buy a pestle and mortar for this very purpose.

Jim laughed. "Who's a lucky boy then? I won't be needing one now!"

He put on his reading glasses. The writing on the side of the box was very small.

Oxycodone. Extreme caution must be used when taking this medicine. Do not take if you think you might be pregnant. No more than two tablets in 24 hours. Never share prescription medicines with anyone else.

Jim was feeling elated. I can plan anything, ideas come to me in a flash. A pineapple? Yes, nice touch, Jimbo – that wasn't on your list! He poured himself a glass of whisky then laughed in a rather strange way. Lenny Barnes won't be pregnant, that's for sure and as for giving him an overdose – try stopping me. No matter what life throws at me I can handle it. I suppose I'm just one of life's winners.

"Are you listening, Lenny Barnes? No-one gets the better of James W Foster!"

Chapter 17

Charles Greenwood

Charles opened the front door, slowly, staring at Jim as if he were a stranger…

He wore an anxious, frightened expression. Toast crumbs and a streak of marmalade were visible on the front of his dark green jumper. His snowy white hair hadn't been combed or washed for days. Jim noticed Charles' hands, they were shaking; he gripped the door handle as if ready and waiting to flee back inside.

"It's only me Charles, nothing to worry about – I have a present for you. As usual, I got carried away in the farm shop, I bought too much fruit, most of it needs to be eaten by tomorrow. So, how about a nice ripe pineapple? I'll cut it up for you, shall I? They can be messy devils…"

Charles nodded; he looked confused but nevertheless smiled and invited Jim inside.

"Are you the new home-help?" he asked.

"Well, I suppose I can be, if you insist!"

Jim shook his head, oh dear, he's getting worse by the day.

He placed the pineapple on a wooden chopping board, once he'd removed the outer layer, he proceeded to cut it into small pieces. The juicy, sugary fruit was put into two deep cereals bowls then covered with cling-film; one went into the fridge, the other left on the worktop.

The moment Charles turned to stare out of the window, Jim put one foil strip (containing ten of Olivia's painkillers) into a kitchen drawer. The tea-towel remained where he'd left it, folded neatly on the worktop, next to the bowl of pineapple. Now, due to Jim's lively imagination, things were starting to warm up. He felt excited, he loved creating chaos, it was like a drug.

Fifteen minutes after Jim's departure Charles would have no recollection of his visit...

"Hi, Olivia, do forgive me for ringing you but I have to ask, any news from the hospital?"

Olivia sounded chirpy and relaxed.

"Well, Jim, you must be psychic! I had a phone call, about an hour ago, from the Radcliffe Infirmary. I'm pencilled in for the 14th. I can hardly believe it – I hope they don't cancel.

"It's very sad, you know, it's only my turn because somebody's died. I happened to be next on the list…"

"I'm very pleased for you, you've had a long wait. Maybe, after the operation, you can stop taking those strong painkillers, I know they make you feel groggy."

"Funny you should mention them, Jim. I've mislaid a whole box of tablets, well, actually they're capsules. I picked them up on Monday from the pharmacy. I can't understand it, I always put them in the same place."

"Oh, my God," replied Jim, "I think I can help you there. Things are starting to make sense."

"Look, I didn't want to say anything but now I feel duty-bound to tell you what I saw. I'm sorry, Olivia, but it's quite distressing. Yesterday, when you were mowing the lawn, I was cleaning the inside of the landing window. Guess who I saw coming out of your backdoor? Only Charles Greenwood! Yes, honestly. It was very odd – there he was, clutching a pineapple and something made of cloth – brightly coloured. I tried to convince myself you'd asked him to pop round to collect something. Perhaps he was confused, he saw you were busy mowing, so he picked up whatever it was and went home."

Jim could hear Olivia's sigh of relief.

"Oh, I'm so glad you told me. Do you know, I couldn't find that tea-towel anywhere?"

She laughed. "Yes, you're right, it is very bright! I'd just taken it out of the airing cupboard and as for the pineapple, well, I thought I must be going mad. I suppose I better start locking the back door. Poor old Charles, I didn't know he was that bad."

For once, Jim could tell the truth.

"A few days ago, I spotted him in the front garden, weeding. It was pouring with rain and he was still wearing his pyjamas. He waved and shouted, 'Good evening, Jack'. It was eight o'clock in the morning. Naturally, I encouraged him to go back inside. I managed to calm him down – once he'd changed into dry clothing. I stayed with him for a while, made us both a cup of strong coffee. I think I needed the caffeine more than he did…"

"That was sweet of you, Jim. However, I wonder why he was rooting around in my kitchen drawer? I can't imagine what he was looking for. He must have helped himself to the painkillers. Let's hope he hasn't swallowed any."

Jim frowned and looked concerned even though they were speaking on the telephone and he couldn't be seen by anyone.

"Oh crikey, I think we'd better go round immediately. We'll go together, speak to Charles, see if we can find out what's been going on."

On their return, Olivia insisted on opening a bottle of Riesling (too sweet for Jim's liking) then, without further ado, a large box of Black Magic appeared.

An unopened box of chocolates would always be kept at the back of the kitchen cupboard; Olivia knew, once opened, she'd eat the lot. She'd bought them in order to cheer herself up, after her hip operation.

Speaking to Charles had been a daunting experience. When questioned, he'd behaved like a frightened child, staring at the floor, then without warning, burst into tears. Jim and Olivia felt uncomfortable, unsure what to do next…

"I'm awfully sorry," he said, dabbing his eyes.

"I didn't know I'd taken them, please believe me. I can't even remember going into your kitchen. Whatever must you think of me?"

Olivia felt obliged to give him a motherly hug.

Only ten capsules were found, which was hardly surprising: the remaining twenty were inside a sock at the back of Jim's airing cupboard, hidden behind a pile of snowy white bath towels.

Olivia insisted, they must search all the obvious places. When no more capsules were found they agreed, Charles must have thrown them into the pedal bin. No-one was prepared to rifle though discarded meals, damp tea-bags, eggshells or other unmentionables in order to find out!

Fortunately for Jim, Charles seemed blissfully unaware of his previous visit. The poor chap knew nothing about painkillers, a missing tea-towel or a bowl of pineapple pieces found on the top shelf of his fridge.

Olivia looked at Jim and smiled warmly.

"Charles made an excellent job of cutting up my pineapple, did you notice? Bless him. I'm surprised he didn't chop off a finger…"

"From now on, Olivia, we'll have to keep an eye on him. Dementia is a terrible thing. We can only do our best. According to Charles, his son works in Paris – some European bank – sounds impressive. It's Robert, isn't it, the son? I assume you have his telephone number, just in case?"

"Oh, yes. I've telephoned Robert once or twice. He has a French wife, Suzette, from the Loire valley. She has a very sexy accent, you'd like her. Tres chic as the French like to say."

Chapter 18

The Lure of Money

Once home, Jim poured himself a whisky then made it a double.

So far, things had worked out according to plan. Having Charles Greenwood living next-door was a real bonus. Charles could be called upon (at some point in the future) if the police were asking awkward questions or an alibi was required. No doubt the poor soul would back Jim's story, no matter how bizarre, without blinking an eyelid.

Jim sniggered in a rather immature way.

"When imagination was handed out, I must have been at the front of the queue!"

He could fill Charles' muddled head with all sorts of frightening images: monsters, evil spirits, dead bodies – oh yes, especially dead bodies – then tell him there was no need to worry.

'It's alright, Charles, don't panic – it was only one of your nasty old dreams. Let's have a nice cup of tea, shall we?'

Once Olivia was out of the way (in hospital for ten days) he could 'join the dots.' Lenny Barnes was a dead man walking. What a fool, he should have known better. Getting on the wrong side of Jim Foster always ended in tears.

Jim relaxed in his favourite chair, stretched and yawned. It wasn't long before he fell into a deep and restless sleep. The wine and the whisky had taken their toll...

Celia had insisted on taking Olivia to the Radcliffe infirmary.

"It's not necessary or appropriate for Jim to get involved. I've known you far longer. Anyway, any medical stuff is best kept between us ladies."

Olivia didn't argue or bother to reply. She didn't care who drove her to the hospital, all she wanted was a new hip and a chance to become pain-free.

"Lenny? It's Jim Foster. I think we've got unfinished business. Will Friday evening suit you? My place, drinks at seven-thirty?"

"Sorry, Jim, I'll have to ring you back, I'm in the middle of something important."

He was taken aback; he hadn't expected to hear from Jim, not yet and certainly not when he was in the office.

Lenny was anything but happy.

Jim sounded too confident, bossy, he was sending a message – I'm in charge now! Lenny felt worried, had he gone too far? He should be making the arrangements, pulling all the strings, not Jim.

Lenny's day had gone from bad to worse…

He'd just returned from showing a thoroughly unpleasant couple a run-down two-bedroomed semi. Unsurprisingly, they'd hated it. However, it was the only property available within their meagre budget.

Fifty-eight-year-old Mrs Higgins (from Swindon) was a huge, bossy woman who'd consumed a whole bag of Werther's Originals whilst complaining non-stop about the size of the rooms.

"Well, Les," she'd said, through nicotine-stained teeth, "this is all down to you. It's time you got off your arse and did some overtime then we might be able to afford a decent place, not one of them tiny rabbit hutches!

"If I had my way, you'd give up betting on the gee-gees and going down the pub with them stupid mates of yours!"

Les was pushed roughly towards the exit.

Without saying a further word, Grace Higgins followed her skinny, hen-pecked husband through the front door of Barnes and Hornet, hardly noticing the pouring rain. It would be difficult to find another woman with such an ill-fitting name; there was nothing graceful about Grace Higgins.

Lenny Scowled. "Oh my God, who are these bloody people? Some days, I hate this job. If I was married to that miserable cow, I'd be gambling too, and going down the pub, yeah, anything to get away from her…"

He picked up the office phone, hoping to sound more confident than he felt.

"Sorry about that, Jim, I was right in the middle of something – what a nightmare. One of them days, I'm afraid.

"Yeah, Friday will do nicely. You'll have the money, as promised? No funny business?"

"Yes, of course I will, that's why I rang you, cash, like we agreed. Oh, by the way Lenny – don't go getting any silly ideas. Ten grand, that's it, a one-off payment. Come on your own and tell no-one or the deal's off."

Friday evening was cold and crisp, the pale-yellow moon appearing bigger and brighter than usual. Lenny looked up, millions of stars like tiny pin-pricks littered the navy-blue sky. A helicopter flew low, skimming the rooftops of Bridgeford. Could it be police officers, searching for someone with their state-of-the-art thermal cameras?

After leaving his car keys beside the toaster, Lenny picked up the front door key, set the burglar alarm, then locked the front door. A brisk walk would be beneficial – Gallica Rose was only ten minutes on foot and he could certainly do with the exercise, he was getting flabby.

He smirked. I can get drunk too, if I walk round. I bet old Foster's got some good stuff. No cheap supermarket booze for him...

Lenny was feeling buoyant, ten thousand pounds (cash) was coming his way. What would he do with it? No contest. He'd always fancied a bright red Alfa Romeo. He'd seen just the car he wanted, advertised online. Not far away either, a small garage, just off the A40.

His second-hand Mercedes must be worth six grand, not a scratch on it, low mileage too. For sixteen thousand quid he could buy himself a nice motor, even without touching his savings. He'd take a ride over to Gloucester the following day and take a look at it.

Steve Hornet wouldn't mind, he might even encourage him to go early if things were quiet. Steve was a good bloke.

After dealing with 'fatty and skinny' (Mr and Mrs Higgins) he could do with a treat.

Fancy Jim asking me round for drinks. Bit odd – bit flash! I've got him rattled alright, perhaps he's scared of me. He probably thinks I'll be blackmailing him for evermore!

He laughed. "Oh, yes," he whispered, "and if he thinks that, he'll be dead right!"

Lenny was out of breath, he shouldn't be, not at his age. He decided, there and then, he ought to take more exercise. Lenny's dad, Ernie, had been grossly overweight. He must avoid following the 'Barnes family trend', no exercise, an expanding waistline and a fatal heart attack in your early sixties. Ernie's father and his older brother Sid, has succumbed to the same fate.

Life was good. He was determined to be the first Barnes to buck the trend and live to be one hundred! A brisk walk, each evening, would do him a power of good. He enjoyed being outside in the dark; it felt invigorating, exciting…

Tomorrow evening, once he'd been over to see the Alfa, he'd go for another walk, but he'd choose a different route, he'd take a wander across Fosdyke Park. The gravel path had just been completed so you could walk around the perimeter without getting muddy shoes.

Lenny scowled, Fosdyke Park. The very place where he'd seen Jim and Shelly acting like soppy teenagers. They'd been searching for conkers and laughing as they ran hand in hand through the autumn leaves. Fancy kissing Shelly on the lips, in public, at his age! Pathetic.

With their fancy matching scarves, they looked as if they were taking part in a photo-shoot for some glossy magazine – Vogue, perhaps – an advertisement for top-end country clothing. What was the name? Oh yes, Burberrys.

What if they'd been seen by his mates? He'd never live it down. Even now, it made his blood boil.

By moonlight, Gallica Rose was a very different place, Lenny thought it looked creepy. Its dark, thatched roof and small windows reminded Lenny of something from a once feared fairy tale, Hansel and Gretel.

Maybe his greed was making him feel uneasy. Deep-down he admired Jim, a self-made millionaire, a clever bloke. Lenny shivered, he wasn't sure why but he wanted nothing more than to turn around and run back home…

Too late, the front door opened.

"Ah, good evening, Lenny, right on time. I see it's a full moon, what a lovely evening for a walk. *Do come in…*"

Lenny felt scared, he had a bad feeling – a sixth sense – something truly awful was about to happen. Why did Jim have a strange expression on his face? Why were his pupils enlarged and his cheeks flushed?

He was smiling far too much and behaving in a weird, 'chummy' sort of way. Certainly not the ice-cold welcome you'd expect to receive if you'd come round to extract a great deal of cash from an unfortunate victim.

"Now then, Lenny, before we get down to business you might like to try something special. I bought myself a superb single malt, *'Glenrothes Speyside',* it's loved by the Royal family. Over one hundred pounds a bottle. I know what you're thinking – such extravagance!

"Well, when one lives alone it's something to look forward to, especially at this time of year when one is obliged to turn on the central heating or light the wood burning stove...

"I've been looking for a reason to open it, can I tempt you?"

Lenny loved a glass of whisky but still, one hundred quid a bottle? Oh, well, it might steady his nerves.

"Yeah, why not? Cheers, Jim, I'll have a double if that's not too greedy. It's not every day I'm offered such classy stuff."

Jim smiled but his following comment made Lenny feel even more uncomfortable.

"Life is very short, Lenny, we must make the most of it. One never knows when the grim reaper might call – even for you, young man – in the prime of life..."

Lenny shivered, why was Jim being so weird? One minute he was smiling, offering him a single malt then the next he was talking about death.

Jim turned his back on Lenny in order to prepare the drinks.

"Oh, by the way, if you look inside that brown Jiffy bag, over there on the coffee table, you'll find the cash. It's all there, but feel free to count it, I won't be offended."

Lenny moved towards the coffee table, a sudden movement outside the patio doors caught his eye.

"Oh, we've got company – guess what I can see? A red fox, it's beautiful. Just look at that tail! It's eating something, yes, looks like a fallen apple from your orchard – oh, dear, I hope it don't get belly-ache."

Lenny laughed but Jim didn't respond.

Whilst Lenny's back was turned, admiring the fox, Jim took the ready-made concoction from the drinks' cabinet. A cheap supermarket whisky was good enough for a such a common, working-class man. Earlier in the day three of Olivia's Oxycodone capsules had been snipped open and their contents squeezed into the glass.

Lenny checked the wad of fifty-pound notes then returned the Jiffy bag to the coffee table. Jim handed over Lenny's drink.

"Oh, cheers mate, your very good health.

"To be honest, Jim, I'm surprised you agreed to my demands, I expected you to put up more of a fight! You can't blame me for trying, can you? Everyone knows you're loaded."

Lenny relaxed, looked across at Jim then winked. Oh, yes, he'd soon be driving that beautiful red Alfa Romeo!

How wrong could he be?

"Can I ask you something, Jim? All that funny business with your lady-friend, Georgia de Vere, what the hell was that about? Frightened of some old Victorian book, eh? Made you sound like a right idiot, what a plonker!"

Lenny laughed, loudly, he was enjoying himself; he could be as rude as he liked, Jim could do nothing about it.

"Now then, matey, as you well know, I didn't appreciate you getting your grubby paws on my ex-missus – you stepped in a bit lively there. Anyway, what's ten-grand to the likes of you?"

Lenny was pushing his luck, becoming over-confident, some might say, disrespectful: he finished his drink.

Jim nodded, but failed to reply – why bother?

The empty glass landed silently on the thick burgundy carpet. Lenny slumped over, making a weird nasal sound, Jim felt uneasy. The volume increased; it was frightening – it certainly wasn't snoring – it was more like the roar of a caged beast.

Jim used cable ties to keep Lenny's hands together – much easier to obtain than a pair of handcuffs.

The internet sites seemed to provide only pink fluffy handcuffs (in the adult section) the thought of which made Jim chuckle, even now.

A large, transparent freezer bag was pulled over Lenny's head then secured with thick garden twine (hidden in Jim's trouser pocket for this very purpose). Lenny's legs began to kick out, his eyes looked enormous and his expression became one of stark terror. Jim felt repulsed by Lenny's face; he should have selected an opaque supermarket carrier bag instead.

This grotesque scene would stay with him for the remainder of his life...

Jim had no desire to witness Lenny's death (it would be gruesome and upsetting) so instead, he poured himself another glass of Glenrothes and carried it through to the study. He closed the curtains. The night air was cool, he shivered (nerves, perhaps) and turned up the thermostat.

"Ah, here we are," he whispered, gazing at his laptop, "boutique hotels."

I wonder what Alan Bamford and Bertie Fielding are getting up to? I'm tempted to take Olivia up to the Lakes – when she's made a full recovery. Anyway, a change of scenery is always good for one's health.

We could stay with them, in their lovely stone cottage. What was it called? Ah, yes, The Hidden Tarn. As far as I know, no-one else is aware of their delightful love nest. He smirked.

"Oh, boy, I'm going to have some fun with this!"

Jim lacked empathy and refused to change his outdated views on same-sex relationships or the modern world in general.

His thoughts continued apace. With just a few words I could destroy everything. I could ruin their hopes, their dreams, their cosy little life. Naturally, I'd play the innocent. I'd comment on Alan's surname then mention our neighbour, the widow, *Celia Bamford.*

Poor Alan, he'll probably have a panic attack then turn white as a sheet: he'll hurry back to the kitchen and into the welcoming arms of dear Bertie…

Jim sniggered, what a silly couple they are.

No doubt Olivia (poor woman) will be surprised and confused. And me? I'll try (using my excellent acting skills) to mimic her behaviour.

"Yes, it would be cruel and spiteful to reveal their secret life, but even so, I'd enjoy every moment."

Jim wondered how Olivia would behave on their return. Would she feel duty-bound to spill the beans? Perhaps she'd rush over to tell Celia about Alan's new and happy life – let's face it – who could resist?

Jim clearly didn't know Olivia at all. On discovering Alan was alive and in a loving relationship, she'd probably say nothing to Celia or anyone else. Olivia, unlike Jim, was a good person who radiated kindness and empathy.

Jim checked his watch, stretched and yawned. How time flies when you're on the internet. Lenny must be dead by now – still, there's only one way to find out!

Lifting Lenny's 'still warm' body into the chest freezer hadn't been easy. He'd had to stand on the kitchen steps then ease it slowly over the side. How fortunate Lenny Barnes wasn't a grossly overweight young man, that would have made things very difficult. Jim eyes were set firmly on Lenny's chest thus avoiding the merest glimpse of the hideous human face concealed within the freezer bag...

Stark memories of St Christopher's House rushed into Jim's head. Molly's private room (complete with sea-view) had cost an arm and a leg. It didn't matter – Jim could afford it – money wasn't a problem back then or now. He tried to picture her face, not in death but as a vision of loveliness, walking down the aisle on their wedding day. All he managed to conjure up was a ghostly image – like a photographic negative –with blurred features.

Was Molly destined to have a starring-role in an all too frequent nightmare? Might this be his earthly torment, arranged by some higher authority? In his dream, Molly's face was a whiter shade of pale, her vibrant green eyes full of fear and trepidation. Her once elegant wedding dress was filthy and covered with rotting leaves, spiders and cobwebs. It was Molly's terrified expression that worried him the most – had she guessed what was to come?

Jim had murdered his wife without a second thought, he deserved no peace of mind or guilt-free dreams...

Jim sighed. Petechial Haemorrhaging. Oh, my God, what a mouthful. Those wretched words will haunt me until my dying day. Jim had been assured by Molly's doctor that in her case (due to poor health and the effects of Warfarin) the tiny red and purple spots seen beneath the skin were perfectly normal, nothing to cause concern.

Now that Lenny had been suffocated too, albeit in a very different way, those much-hated words had resurfaced. Why was life so damned complicated? It wasn't his fault – people made him do bad things.

In a healthy young man (like Lenny) Petechial Haemorrhaging would certainly ring alarm bells. Suffocation would be suspected and investigated, immediately.

Jim laughed. His confidence restored.

"No problem, that's never going to happen! It will be as if Lenny Barnes has disappeared off the face of the earth. By the time they dig him up, in a hundred years or so, I'll be long gone."

The chest freezer was in the garage. He'd been on the point on having it taken away; he didn't need it, not for one person, thank goodness he'd changed his mind. Anyway, Lenny wouldn't be in there for long…

The following morning, Jim could be seen walking casually around his rear garden, looking at this and that, but in reality, searching for just the right spot.

On reaching the orchard he hesitated, deep in thought. In one corner there were several large, abandoned rocks left over from the poorly constructed rockery. He'd noticed them, of course, but their usefulness had yet to register. Someone had over-estimated wildly, their ineptitude could be to his advantage. No-one would be surprised or take any notice whatsoever if he decided to have a tidy-up and change things around.

Olivia was in hospital, awaiting her new hip and Charles Greenwood, well, Jim could spin him a rare old tale – silly old fool.

Jim shivered and hurried back inside; he'd left his jumper on the back of a kitchen chair. The wind had veered to the north-east making him feel chilled to the bone.

He checked his watch, twenty past eleven, time to turn on his excellent new coffee machine.

Jim looked deep in thought, then smiled. Lenny won't mind spending eternity in a shallow grave, there's far worse places, and I do have a rather splendid garden.

I hope my back doesn't play up – I'm getting a bit old for heavy digging. I shall have to buy some of that ibuprofen gel, just in case.

Nothing must affect my golf swing – my handicap is down to eleven – that's very good for a chap my age. That reminds me, I must ask Celia about Bridgeford Golf Club. I believe it's one of the finest in the Cotswolds. No doubt she'll offer to show me round – pretending we're more than good friends – maybe, but only in her dreams! When her playing partners see me, they'll be green with envy. I shall certainly set a few hearts aflutter…

For the second time that morning, Jim looked in the hall mirror, combed his hair and smiled at his reflection. He winked.

"Still got it!" he whispered.

Chapter 19

Bonfire Night

The rapid fall in temperature and long dark evenings suited Jim's devious plans...

Downstairs curtains and blinds (and even better, bedroom curtains) would be closed. His neighbours in the Evesham Road would be snuggling down in front of the television – central heating turned up – blissfully unaware of his furtive, not to say, highly illegal, behaviour.

As they enjoyed a tasty takeaway or demolished a box of chocolates, Jim would be digging a very large hole (beside the fruit trees) away from prying eyes. A grave, made to measure, for local estate agent, Lenny Barnes.

Since murdering Lenny, Jim made a point of spending more time in the garden, an hour here, forty minutes there, it was always good to appear busy. Close neighbours, seeing him loading up the car and making frequent visits to the local tip would be impressed by his boundless energy and ceaseless enthusiasm.

Now they'd seen him in the garden (even when the light was fading) his movements and any eccentricities would probably be ignored…

The dahlias had been cut down and covered with a thick layer of compost, perfect for keeping frost at bay. Now the cosmos had finished dropping their tiny seeds, he could pull them out and add them to the growing pile of garden waste.

Jim looked, but found no evidence of a compost heap. He didn't want one anyway, tricky things, prone to smelly, slimy grass cuttings if you didn't get things right!

Several brittle branches had snapped off and blown down, victims of the autumn winds; he'd gathered them up and formed some semblance of a bonfire. November 5th, just a few days away.

As multi-coloured fireworks lit up the night sky and bangers made children jump, Jim would be having fun in a very different, more macabre sort of way.

He'd invite Charles round on the 5th, they could make an evening of it. He'd buy a large box of sparklers and attach a few Catherine wheels to the fence – something to enjoy as they stood beside the roaring bonfire. He'd pick up some tasty sausage rolls from Temptations and warm up some soup – Charles would enjoy that too. Jim wasn't being altruistic, he was thinking only of himself: Charles, confused but standing by his side at moments of great importance could only be a good thing. Planting 'false memories' in Charles' addled brain would be easy, the poor chap believed everything Jim told him.

He'd made an effigy of Guy Fawkes and placed it on top of the bonfire, it was rather amateurish but it wouldn't matter once the fire was ablaze!

It was wearing a bright red knitted scarf...

If all went according to plan, Lenny's frozen body would be taking its final journey the previous evening. Jim would squeeze him (stiff though he was) into the wheelbarrow and off they'd go, merrily, up to the orchard.

Perhaps he'd whistle a jolly tune. Yes, 'Hi ho, hi ho, it's off to work we go'. Jim laughed. Sometimes I'm no less than an evil genius.

Lenny would be wearing the same bright red knitted scarf – plus something else – Jim's old gardening hat...

Prior to burial, the red scarf would be removed from Lenny's ice-cold body and tucked into Jim's coat pocket. Later, it would be returned to the guy's neck. Charles would be convinced (no matter what he may have seen) there was only one 'body', made from a couple of unwanted cushions, odds and sods, a mask and some old clothes.

"Confused? Poor devil, he might be!"

Dressing the body in a way that matched the effigy had been a clever stroke.

Jim smiled his creepy, devious smile.

I must resist the temptation to make a little cross out of twigs and place it by Lenny's grave. We did that when I was a child after one of our beloved pets died...

Once Bonfire night was over, a new rockery would emerge – right on top of the grave. The following spring Lenny would be no more than a distant memory...

"Thanks Jim, I've had a lovely time. Your bonfire party and the pretty fireworks have made me feel young again. Though it's a pity you didn't provide a few glamorous ladies – for later on!"

Jim laughed and put his arm around Charles' shoulders.

"Oh, Charles, you do surprise me, you cheeky boy, I thought you were such a gentleman..."

They were behaving like a couple of good friends, enjoying each other's company.

"I watched you, Jim – as you wheeled the guy up to the top of the garden – then I lost sight of you in the orchard. I was closing the bedroom curtains, it gets dark so early, doesn't it? I couldn't stand there, waiting for you to reappear as I wanted to watch a gardening programme on, um, something or other. Whatever was it? Oh, yes, I remember now, pruning roses…"

"Well, I can assure you, Charles, you didn't miss anything!"

Jim offered Charles another hot sausage roll. They'd returned to the kitchen as the bonfire was nearly extinguished and the night air had a dampness about it which seemed to penetrate their clothing.

"Can I ask you something, Jim? I know I get confused but the effigy you were pushing around in the wheelbarrow looked much taller, his legs were longer and his face, well, it looked more realistic. If you don't mind me saying, the guy you put on the bonfire was smaller, nowhere near as life-like. I wonder, did you decide to make another one?"

Jim was taken aback by Charles' inquisitive nature. Did Dementia manifest itself in that way?

Good days and bad? He decided, there and then, he'd have to be on his guard. Still, now the body was buried, he could relax, all would be well.

"Well done, Charles, I wondered if you'd notice, you're very observant.

"Yes, although my first effort may have looked more life-like, it wasn't very good – far too tall – cumbersome, one might say. As I lifted the poor thing onto the bonfire, a leg fell off so I shortened his legs, but I'm pleased to say he didn't complain!

"That's why I took it up to the orchard, I was off to the shed, I had to make a few alterations."

Charles laughed, thanking Jim once again for a most enjoyable evening.

After fastening his coat against the prevailing wind, he left by the back door, carrying with him the remaining sausage rolls…

Chapter 20

A Short Break

Winter had been surprisingly mild with hardly a flake of snow, well, nothing south of Dumfries and Galloway...

When March arrived, bringing warm sunshine and feelings of hope, Jim had a new-found confidence about him. Cyclamen flowers were visible (poking through the dark soil) in shades of pink, mauve and white.

The week before Christmas, he'd spent hours in the garden planting hundreds of bulbs: anemones, miniature tulips, tiny white narcissus and assorted crocuses.

However, these bulbs were not in the borders or under trees: Jim had been determined to fill every gap in the new rockery. He'd moved numerous large, heavy rocks, dragging them along until he could place them on top of Lenny's burial plot.

He felt no guilt, why should he? Lenny Barnes had over-stepped the mark. Give in to blackmail? Not likely!

Olivia's hip-replacement had been a great success. Short walks were possible and later in the year she'd be travelling to California to meet her first grandchild, Marcus. Due to the size of the baby (over nine pounds) the birth had been traumatic. Melissa had declared, 'Never again' and meant it...

Jim sat in his favourite armchair (lap-top turned on) admiring photographs of The Hidden Tarn, the charming boutique hotel owned and run by Alan Bamford and Bertie Fielding.

It was Olivia who'd suggested taking long country walks together, after all, the Cotswolds had so much more to offer than shopping. It wasn't long before a warm friendship developed; they enjoyed one another's company and shared many interests.

Ah, but would Olivia be prepared to go on holiday with him? Jim smiled, knowing the answer.

Yes, of course she would. He assumed any woman in her right mind would jump at the chance.

He pressed print – then watched excitedly as details appeared.

Picking up a pair of scissors he removed the final paragraph as it displayed the owners' names and 'that' photograph: the newly married couple, sitting together on a dry-stone wall, right outside their delightful, white-washed cottage.

Olivia mustn't see Alan Bamford's name it would ruin everything and spoil all the fun!

If Olivia should notice something was amiss, he'd merely shrug and say the page became caught up in the printer and as he'd run out of A4 paper, he'd been unable to print off another copy.

Once again, Jim Foster – murderer, liar and sociopath – had an answer for everything…

"No, Olivia, I insist, it's my idea, so it's my treat; I wouldn't have it any other way. You know me, chivalrous to the end!"

Olivia leant over and gave him a kiss on the cheek, in a friendly but certainly not suggestive way...

"Oh, bless you, Jim. I haven't had a holiday for five years – I'm looking forward to it already."

Jim wished he was taking Shelly to the Lakes but it would be pointless, she wouldn't fit in with his carefully crafted plans. She was alluring, vivacious and fun to be with, in fact the prospect of spending three uninterrupted nights in her bed was driving him mad – but he must be patient, level-headed, not driven by lust.

One day, he'd whisk her away, anywhere she wanted – it would be their very own holiday of a lifetime. No expense spared. He'd bought a well-chosen present for her already, with the sole intention of putting it on the bed in their hotel room. Choosing perfume for a lady, someone he'd been dating for such a short time could be problematic.

Georgia de Vere had loved, *Lime, Basil and Mandarin,* by Jo Malone. Would Shelly also appreciate its subtle tones?

Jim's imagination was running away with him. After a shower Shelly would apply the body crème then climb into bed and cuddle up beside him. Perhaps, if she was behaving in a flirtatious mood, he'd be invited to massage a little of the body crème into her skin…

Jim scowled. If he so much as suggested booking a double room, Olivia would run a mile; she was still in love with Guy, her late husband. Jim knew he could never be more than a friend. How could he compete with the memory of a dead man?

He was aware that his plan to humiliate Celia would need the co-operation of an unsuspecting Olivia. He was like a dog with a bone, he wouldn't relax until Celia got her comeuppance. One day he'd make her apologise for her sarcastic comments. Her eyes had been blazing when she mentioned Georgia de Vere's break-in. What had Celia said?

'Poor little Jimmy Foster, scared of a tatty old book, The Fortune Teller's Handbook.'

He sighed. He'd just have to take Shelly to the Lakes at a later date. Right now, he simply couldn't resist causing mischief. Life was far too short to be nice…

Ever since Lenny's disappearance, Shelly had been subdued, distracted; she'd turned down a shopping trip and an overnight stay in London. He'd been showing off, trying to impress her.

"I know what you ladies enjoy – buying shoes and handbags. Well, darling, let's have fun, we'll buy up the whole of Oxford Street! You can have anything you like…"

He'd been surprised then angry with her. He could hardly believe it; how dare she turn him down! She would have adored The Tudor Rose it was one of London's oldest and finest hotels.

Shelly was worried. Lenny could be a pig at times and they were divorced but she still cared for him – just in a different sort of way. Something was wrong, very wrong. People like Lenny Barnes, who ran a successful business and displayed no outward signs of alcohol abuse or family feuds, don't normally go missing. His business partner, Steve Hornet, voiced what everyone else was thinking.

"Do you know, Shelly, I've got a horrible feeling he's been murdered – some gang related stuff, down in London – I bet we never see him again. He's always had a dodgy side and you know it."

Shelly burst into tears. Steve took her by the hand and led her across the road to the Coach and Horses where he ordered two glasses of brandy; the sympathetic landlord understood Shelly's tears. His customers had discussed Lenny Barnes' mysterious disappearance on many occasions. When Steve tried to pay for the drinks the landlord shook his head – no – they were on the house.

Ever since Lenny's disappearance Steve had been plagued by a tension headache. What the hell was going on? The response from the Police had been lukewarm which is often the case when someone disappears. It was time the Police got their act together:

were extensive enquiries being made, back in the East End? Steve sighed, he doubted it…

Lenny wouldn't go off and start a new life without telling his mum; they were and always had been, very close. Lily Barnes rang Shelly on a daily basis – she was a bag of nerves. Lenny had enemies in the East End, but that was in his youth, years ago, he'd finished with petty crime, surely. That was the only the reason Ernie Barnes had moved his family to the Cotswolds, to make a fresh start. Besides, if Lenny returned to London, no matter what the reason, who would he contact first? His mum, of course…

Jim was deep in thought. Celia would be flabbergasted when told of Alan's new and happy life. He'd deceived her for years; some might say they'd been living a lie. Had Alan been in a relationship with Bertie whilst married to Celia? Jim smirked, oh my word, no wonder she's frustrated! That's why she stroked my thigh and tried to seduce me. Perhaps she's still a virgin! Still, any normal woman would be sexually aroused by a man like me. I'm probably the most attractive man Celia has ever seen.

Jim poured himself another mug of coffee; his attitude had softened, somewhat...

Fancy coming out of the closet and admitting you're gay – it can't have been easy after nine years of marriage. It takes guts, so well done Alan. Would Celia be prepared to forgive him and admire his courage?

After settling down in Bridgeford, Celia informed everyone (with a voice choked by emotion) that her husband, Alan, had died in tragic circumstances, whilst working abroad. She couldn't talk about it – it was far too painful.

When the truth came out, people would gossip. Had Celia known, or perhaps suspected her husband was gay? Jim chuckled, the future was looking rosy, this story could run and run...

Once they'd been to the Lakes and Olivia discovered Alan Bamford was alive and kicking, she'd feel obliged to inform Celia – who could resist? If Olivia refused to speak out (trying to protect her friend) then he'd be happy to oblige. Would Celia be brave enough to recount Alan's fascinating story to her closest friends?

He shook his head. *Um, no, perhaps I'd better do it for her…*

He'd have a coffee in Temptations, making a point of talking to Ruby and Alice then spread a few salacious rumours.

Jim was convinced the twins were more than a little in love with him. No doubt they would digest his every word whilst gazing longingly into his deep blue eyes…

However, Celia would have to tell them something. Her expression and demeanour would suggest something was on her mind, however, telling the truth would only serve to underline her previous lies and deception…

Jim shook his head, oh dear, poor old Celia, how would she cope? He hadn't decided how and when he would drop the bombshell…

Alan and Bertie had been so welcoming, so kind. On arrival, Alan grabbed their suitcases and whisked them up to the second floor – adjoining rooms – numbers eight and ten.

The décor was superb; art nouveau wallpaper, pastel colours and large comfortable sofas. The bathrooms were delightful: white suite with burgundy tiles and cream-coloured carpets.

After unpacking, they returned to the lounge; someone had turned on a dusty old CD player, jazz was playing in the background. Jim nodded approvingly.

"Ah, yes, Dizzy Gillespie, I think."

Bertie walked in, carrying a large tray. He smiled, shyly.

"You mentioned you were hungry so here's a little treat for you. We don't serve an evening meal until seven so as it's just after three, I thought a cream tea might be appreciated. I made the scones half an hour ago, they're still warm."

Olivia and Jim looked at each other, they could think of nothing they'd like more. Olivia smiled warmly at Bertie.

"Oh, Bertie, that's absolutely perfect. How very sweet of you."

Bertie smiled shyly, then returned to the kitchen to join Alan.

Jim felt irritated: all this 'Bertie and Alan' stuff, huh, pathetic. In my day, it was always Mr and Mrs, or in this case, Mr and Mr.

As yet, there had been no mention of surnames, still, no rush, he'd bide his time. He'd need to steer the conversation in a particular direction: he could do it – he could do anything. He'd catch them unawares, he'd say something quite innocently, something to knock their socks off!

The following morning, at eight-thirty, Jim sat in reception waiting for Olivia. More art nouveau, more exposed beams. The room was bright and airy, decorated in shades of pink and cream. The left-hand wall was covered with black and white prints by

221

Aubrey Beardsley. Not to my liking – thought Jim – rather effeminate, reminds me of a tart's boudoir. He smirked. Not that I've even been in one.

This was the only downstairs room to give a hint as to the whereabouts of the hidden tarn. The early morning sun was dazzling, Jim could see the glare off the water, a mere two hundred metres away. He shielded his eyes. Idyllic was the only word capable of describing such a view: gentle rolling hills backed by purple-topped mountains and if that wasn't enough, a rainbow appeared just as he walked towards the window.

Make the most of it, boys, your perfect little world is about to come tumbling down...

Jim checked his watch, eight-forty, where the hell was Olivia? She was ten minutes late.

Behind the desk was a collection of photographs. Jim smiled his devious smile, liking what he saw.

Alan and Bertie in a group photo – names underneath – taken when they were studying at

Cambridge University. Further along the wall, even better, two black and white photos, the boys, wearing 'cap and gown' at their graduation ceremony. This was gold-dust!

It was exciting, a shiver ran down his spine, he must be quick! Within seconds, Jim, phone in hand, had photographed these charming images.

"So sorry, Jim," said a breathless Olivia.

"I was looking for something, a pearl earring. These are my favourite earrings, given to me by Guy, on my fortieth birthday – I had to find it. Anyway, all's well. These carpets are so thick – no wonder it took so long to find it.

"I see you have your phone at the ready, were you about to take some photographs of the view? It's spectacular! How clever you are, thank you for choosing such a lovely place."

He nodded, enthusiastically.

"Oh, thank you, darling, I'm so glad you like it. Yes, the moment I discovered the Hidden Tarn I knew it was the perfect place for my lovely companion."

"Oh, Jim, you're such a charmer. Come on, let's go and have some breakfast. I wonder, do you have plans for today?"

"Well, as the sun is shining, I thought a boat trip on Windermere would be rather nice. I've just been looking in the guidebook, it's ten and a half miles long. There's something very relaxing about a boat trip, don't you think?"

"Definitely. I don't remember the last time I set foot on a boat."

There was a queue, but it was very short. They sat on the top deck, with the wind in their hair; Jim offered Olivia his tartan scarf, she grabbed it eagerly.

"I'm so glad you brought it with you that wind is coming from the north-east. We'll have a coffee when we get back."

An elderly gentleman had a stall selling coffee and doughnuts, they couldn't resist, even though it was no more than two hours since they'd enjoyed Bertie's continental breakfast, croissants and freshly ground coffee.

"Good job we didn't have a cooked breakfast," said Olivia.

"I enjoy a tasty fry-up but it slows you down, fills you up for the rest of the day."

"Do you know what I always say, darling? When you're away from home, eat whatever you fancy, you can always make amends when you get home."

After they'd eaten, they drove to nearby Coniston Water, the site where, in 1967, Donald Campbell met his death. This brave Englishman was attempting to break the world water speed record. His famous jet-engine boat, Bluebird, somersaulted then disintegrated. A catastrophic ending for a national hero. His lucky charm, a small teddy bear, was found amongst the wreckage.

Not far from Coniston cemetery an enterprising shop-owner had filled a large, galvanized bucket with deep red roses, it would have been difficult to ignore them. Olivia insisted on buying two roses: one was placed on Donald Campbell's grave, the other thrown into the murky depths in memory of this charismatic and very likeable Englishman. As the sun went down, they watched, silently, as it floated away...

"They don't make *real* heroes like that anymore," said Jim, looking miserable.

"These days heroes are more likely to be footballers, wannabe celebrities or movie stars. Huge egos, grossly overpaid."

Olivia squeezed his hand. After a brisk walk along the foreshore and with the threat of rain ever present, they hurried back to Jim's car.

Jim looked at the clock, it was two-thirty; he'd been in bed since eleven but he couldn't stop his brain from mulling things over. It was going to be a long night...

He awoke with a start. His heart was racing and he couldn't think where he was. He felt panicky, nauseous.

"No, please – not another nightmare."

Jim had always slept well – that is, until the day he'd murdered Molly, his beloved wife. It was then, and only then, the nightmares began…

Jim shook his head, quite violently, trying to erase a terrifying image of Lenny Barnes. The dream was coming back to him, slowly but in vivid colours.

He'd been sitting in Donald Campbell's jet-engine boat, Bluebird, with Lenny Barnes tucked in neatly behind him. Lenny was dressed as a clown – huge red shoes, a bright yellow suit and a frizzy, ginger wig. His eyes and mouth looked ugly – they'd been enhanced by adding streaks of makeup.

Lenny was pointing at him and shouting in a childish voice…

"Come on, Jimbo, faster, faster! Put your foot down you nincompoop or you'll never break the world

record. We're only doing 300mph! I'll tell Bertie – there'll be no more cream teas for you!"

Lenny was holding *The Fortune Teller's Handbook* and a thick wad of notes (presumably Jim's ten thousand pounds). He kept waving the money in Jim's face. The bright red knitted scarf was tied around Lenny's neck; it was caked with maggots and mud...

Jim heard himself scream but only in his nightmare. It was then he'd woken up – his whole body, damp with sweat. He wouldn't get back to sleep, not after such a terrifying experience. He picked up a book, one of several left on a small shelf. He looked at the title and sighed: *World War Two in Colour.*

"Um, well, that won't be a laugh a minute."

He longed for his own home where he had access to a good stiff drink. Perhaps this holiday hadn't been such a good idea after all. Nevertheless, tomorrow would be a very special day – one never to be forgotten...

Chapter 21

Malevolence

A sociopath gains pleasure from hurting others: in Jim Foster's case, not physically but mentally. The antagonist (always guilt-free) feels powerful, almost God-like as he observes the anguish or embarrassment created for his victims…

Jim and Olivia decided to take advantage of the warm sunshine – it was time to put on their boots and explore the hidden tarn with its bewitching aura. They hurried down the grass-covered slope like a couple of youngsters, laughing, holding hands, surprised by their agility. Jim asked Olivia if her new hip would be able to cope, she just smiled and said it was fine. He was delighted, she appeared to be coping very well.

This unspoilt field of 'set-aside' was surrounded by hawthorn hedging.

Mother nature had supplied an abundance of red poppies, white ox-eye daisies and bright blue cornflowers making it look not only spectacular, but patriotic…

"That was fun," declared Jim, "although running in wellington boots is a little tricky.

"Oh, look, over there, in the oak tree, it's an osprey! Shush, darling, don't move a muscle."

They watched as the huge bird of prey swooped down, grabbed hold of a fish, then took off again, all in one graceful movement. They looked at each other, spellbound…

"How lucky was that," whispered Olivia. "No doubt we could sit here all day, all week, and fail to see anything more beautiful. If only you hadn't left the camera in your room."

"Never mind, darling, it's not something we'll ever forget. This place is almost magical, as if sprinkled with fairy dust."

Olivia gazed at him and chuckled.

"Oh, Jim, how poetic you are!"

He pretended to look coy.

"No, I mean it. Alan and Bertie are very clever boys, they could see its possibilities and snapped it up. Good for them! They've worked so hard, decorated from top to bottom, yes, they're perfectionists. I hope they get lots of enquiries. Being gay must be challenging at times – although, thank goodness, not as much as it once was. We'd certainly recommend The Hidden Tarn, wouldn't we?"

"Oh, yes, of course. Alan and Bertie are adorable. I'm getting hungry just thinking about this evening's meal. You can tell Bertie was a chef, he's amazing. Yesterday's beef in red wine was so tender I thought it must be fillet. Surely not, it would be incredibly expensive for a piece that size! How does he do it? Local meat, local contacts, I suppose."

They'd been sitting in the dining room for no more than five minutes when Bertie appeared, a cheeky smile lighting up his face.

A middle-aged couple from Dorking were sitting at the table by the window, whispering. Jim found them dull and boring although Olivia had spoken to them in her usual friendly way. He sneered – what the hell have they got to whisper about?

He looked at them with contempt in his eyes. Their clothes looked cheap. The lady's grey hair had been permed, very tightly – perhaps it had been adversely affected by the damp weather – it had become very frizzy. He hated it, so old-fashionable, in fact, he hated the pair of them.

"Good evening, everyone," said Bertie.

"I hope you've all had a good day and were able to avoid that heavy shower of rain. I've rarely seen a sky so black."

He looked at Olivia, specifically.

"I saw you and Jim walking down to the tarn – I'm so pleased, we hoped you would.

"Anyway, I've made a traditional roast. I do hope that's to everyone's liking. Naturally, there's a vegetarian alternative…"

The middle-aged couple brightened up, looked towards Jim and Olivia and nodded, excitedly. Olivia had just been informing them of Bertie's culinary skills. Jim smiled too, laying on the charm. Nevertheless, he knew full well what was to come…

"A roast? Yes, that'll do nicely, Bertie, thank you. Olivia and I have been looking forward to this meal all day…"

Jim had complete control of the situation and he was enjoying every moment. Timing was important – he must question Alan when he was busy, when he was least expecting it.

Alan put a sage-green bowl on the table, it contained fresh vegetables: carrots, broccoli and petits pois. He returned with a large oval-shaped platter displaying slices of chicken breast (wafer thin) and golden, crispy roast potatoes. A gravy boat was near at hand.

"Oh, you're spoiling us," remarked Olivia.

"My pleasure," replied Alan and meant it.

"I wonder, would anyone care for a little cranberry sauce? We always say, don't just save it for Christmas!"

Olivia nodded and within minutes Alan reappeared with a dainty little dish, filled with cranberry sauce, a tiny spoon standing in its midst. He placed it next to the gravy boat. Jim looked at Alan in a warm and friendly way.

"You have some rather nice photographs in reception – college days, eh? That brings back a few memories. I couldn't help but notice your surname, Bamford, quite unusual. We have a neighbour called Bamford, don't we?"

"Oh, yes, we do," replied Olivia, excitedly, "she's called Celia Bamford, lives opposite – she's a widow – such a knowledgeable gardener. *Mad about roses…"*

Jim was enjoying himself. That's it, go for it, girl, rub it in – frighten the pants off him.

The lady from Dorking was listening to every word of their conversation whilst pretending to look out of the window. Olivia continued, oblivious to the sheer panic and trauma she was causing…

"I'm sure Celia's husband was called Alan. Yes, of course he was – well fancy that, another Alan Bamford."

Now it was Jim's turn to twist the knife…

"I'm probably being daft but I can see a likeness, honestly. Yes, I know, it's the ginger hair, Celia showed me her wedding photograph. It's incredible – her late husband, Alan, looked so much like you. A little younger, of course!"

Jim chuckled, in a matey sort of way. He took a sideways glance at Alan – oh, yes, he was falling apart – looking terrified!

"I wonder, could there be a family connection somewhere? Are there any mystery cousins you've yet to meet?"

He laughed, heartily, looking straight into Olivia's eyes as if totally unaware of poor Alan's obvious distress.

"Have you seen the wedding photograph, in Celia's living room?"

Olivia was silent for a moment.

"Well, to be honest, Jim, I haven't seen it up close, although I know the one you mean, it's on a small side table. Celia doesn't have many photographs on display so that's probably why I noticed it…"

As they prattled on (ignoring Alan) he said not a word, though he was visibly shaken, his face now as white as a sheet. The moment they'd finished speaking, Alan rushed out of the dining room and into the downstairs bathroom.

Jim and Olivia looked confused: he spoke first, wallowing in the knowledge that he had a captive audience. The couple from Dorking appeared to be in a trance: they'd digested every word, unlike their meal, which by now, must be cold…

Jim struggled to keep a straight face – this bit of nonsense must be the most excitement they'd had for years!

"Goodness me, Olivia, what have we done wrong? It sounds like Alan is vomiting. Did you see his face? He looked terrified; I simply don't understand."

"Oh Jim, how innocent you are! Haven't you worked it out yet? That man is Celia's husband, *the* Alan Bamford – he has to be!

"Alan Bamford is alive and well and living in the Lake District. Oh, my giddy aunt, that's incredible. He ran away from Celia in order to start a new life with Bertie. I wonder, does she know where he is?"

Jim looked serious, pretending to mull things over.

"Oh, dear, I see what you mean. Well, judging by his reaction, definitely not, poor Celia hasn't a clue.

"I suppose she was too proud to tell the truth or too embarrassed to admit her husband was gay.

"She explained Alan's absence by saying he'd died just before she moved to Bridgeford. Well, no-one would question that, would they? It's unlikely she's heard from him since – for all she knows, he might really be dead! Still, we have no choice, she must be told the truth, I'd want to know, wouldn't you?"

"Yes Jim, I would, it's better to know the truth, no matter how much it hurts. You're right, we ought to tell her – however, it's going to be such a shock. We'll have to do it very gently."

Jim sighed and took a deep breath.

"I know it's silly but I'm feeling guilty now – if only I'd chosen a different location or another boutique hotel – who knows…"

Jim looked out of the window as if afraid to meet Olivia's gaze. He had perfected the art of looking miserable.

"Oh, Jim, don't be so silly, you mustn't say that! You're a good man, how could you possibly know? Promise me you'll never say that again."

Jim smiled, weakly.

"Well, I got us into this mess, albeit indirectly, so it's up to me to sort it out. When we get back and after the dust has settled, I'll go round and have a quiet word with Celia. You need not be involved.

"I'll be very discreet, I'll set the scene before leading up to the awkward bit."

Olivia nodded but said not a word. Jim was one in a million, a real gentleman, so good at handling awkward situations. It was much the same with Charles Greenwood, when he'd stolen items from her kitchen. Jim sorted that out too.

Olivia smiled to herself: 'The case of the pineapple, the painkillers and the missing tea towel'. Sounds like a job for Miss Marple…

The gloss had been knocked off their holiday. Sadly, Jim and Olivia, and Alan and Bertie, were no longer able to feel relaxed in each other's company…

Now, instead of wishing they had a few more days here, in this magical hideaway, Olivia was looking forward to going home…

Jim paid the bill, a warm smile lighting up his features. He put his hand on Bertie's shoulder before saying, in a fatherly way:

'Please don't worry about a thing, we've had a lovely time. Your cooking is second to none. Many thanks.'

Despite Jim's words of praise Bertie looked utterly deflated whilst Alan kept out of the way, hiding in the kitchen. There was no mention of the previous night's drama – there was nothing to be said…

The journey home had a melancholy feel about it as if a dark cloud had descended upon them. Jim was unusually quiet so Olivia (having slept very little the previous night) decided to take a nap.

They stopped at the services for coffee, cheeseburger and fries, but even a delicious helping of so-called junk food failed to raise their spirits.

Olivia turned her head and glanced quickly at Jim, hoping he'd assume she was admiring the countryside or gazing at a passing car.

He knew exactly what was going on, she was worried about him. He'd sigh, maybe give a little cough or clear his throat. Looking unhappy wasn't easy, although he was a good actor who'd told numerous friends, 'I've missed my vocation – I should have been on the stage!'

Jim's imagination was working overtime. Yes, a play by William Shakespeare, who else? A demanding role like Falstaff or King Lear.

He smiled, thinking warmly of Molly. Their favourite film had been *Rebecca* – made in 1940 – directed by Alfred Hitchcock. It was no less than a masterpiece. Molly used to tease Jim, saying he would have been perfect as Maxim de Winter, played so passionately by the late Sir Laurence Olivier.

He'd introduced this classic black and white movie to Olivia, she'd thoroughly enjoyed it. Despite its age, it was as fresh and compelling as ever. Jim assumed (incorrectly) every woman on earth would find Maxim de Winter irresistible. He was a man of few words: brooding, secretive, sometimes cruel but

241

unbelievably handsome. He possessed something money could never buy – sexual magnetism.

Jim was miles away when Olivia interrupted his thoughts.

"Hey, are you okay? You're very quiet. Do tell me, what's on your mind?"

Jim's conversations were full of truths, half-truths and downright lies…

"Oh, nothing much, darling. I was thinking about my first dog, Rex, given to me by my father on my eighth birthday. A Springer Spaniel, such an affectionate little chap. Just two years after we got him, he was run over, it broke my heart.

"I could be tempted to buy another dog, it keeps you fit, physically and mentally. There's always someone there when you come home, someone who gives unconditional love.

"What do you think? I know how much you miss Boris, your dear old pug."

Olivia looked at him, affectionately.

"Well, Jim, perhaps one of us should have a dog, I agree, they are very good company.

"I've got an idea, I'll take him for a walk on the bright, sunny days, then it'll be your turn when it's pouring with rain, blowing a gale, snowy or slippery…"

Jim laughed.

"Okay, I get the message…"

Chapter 22

A Tragic Accident

Late one Saturday evening, Alice made a stupid mistake, she lied through her teeth and paid the ultimate price...

Alice and Dave had been to Bognor Regis for the day, Ruby staying at home with Blossom. Neither twin had been to the seaside since their late twenties. Ruby was hurt, why hadn't Dave invited both of them? After all, it wasn't somewhere romantic, it was no more than a bit of fun, a chance to recapture their youth.

On their return, Dave managed to park right outside the cottage. He gave Alice a kiss on the cheek. She whispered something, then burst out laughing. Ruby stood back from the window hoping she hadn't been seen: were they talking about her, were they saying spiteful things? Was Dave saying he was madly in love with Alice?

Dave had no intention of going inside to say hello to Ruby, not likely. It'd been a good day out but due to heavy traffic he was feeling very tired. All he wanted was to get home and relax.

Alice was hyped-up, this had been the best day of her life. Having spent time at the funfair (consuming candy floss, fizzy drinks and a couple of hot dogs) she was behaving like a love-struck teenager. She'd made up her mind, if Dave couldn't make a decision, she'd make one for him; they simply couldn't go on like this. Nevertheless, her opening words were cruel and unnecessary...

"Guess what, Rubes? I won, you lost!

"On the way home, Dave proposed. He wants to marry me, not you. Honestly! He told me to keep it a secret, I'm not to tell anyone, *especially you."*

Alice had been drinking, Ruby could smell alcohol on her breath. Alice swayed a little then walked slowly up the stairs without smiling or saying her usual, 'Nighty-night love, sleep well.'

Ruby had reached breaking point too. Alice would not be marrying Dave – not if she had anything to do with it.

Ruby was warm and comfortable beneath her 13.5 tog duvet. She'd tucked two plump pillows behind her huge body and as usual, a packet of chocolate biscuits was within easy reach. Nevertheless, the waiting seemed endless. For over an hour she'd been listening intently for the familiar creak of a certain floorboard...

Very little of her novel, *The Brixworth Poisoner* (a popular Victorian melodrama) had been absorbed. If questioned, she would struggle to remember anything other than the names of the two main characters, a wealthy landowner, Josiah Barton and his timid wife, Florence...

At last, Alice's snoring ceased (albeit temporarily) it was ten-past-three. Ruby yawned, returned her book to the bedside table then grabbed another biscuit. Not long now. Alice's bladder must be on a timer, every night it's the same old routine, off she goes between three and three-thirty. My bladder has a will of its own, I've no idea when I shall be nipping out to the loo.

Just after midnight, Ruby had tiptoed out of her bedroom, removed the bulb from the table lamp and placed it on her dressing table.

Ruby's bedroom door was no more than a metre from the small oak table. Unlike Alice, she had no need to walk over a creaky floorboard or pass the top of the stairs.

Electricity had been installed as early as 1926, in fact it was one of the first properties in Bridgeford-upon-Avon to receive such a modern marvel. However, it had been impossible to add a light fitting to the landing ceiling due to the huge oak beams.

Ruby must make a decision – would a light touch be enough or a would a hefty shove be required? It didn't really matter, after all, there would be no evidence to suggest her sister had been pushed.

However, there would be numerous broken bones and bruises from the fall…

Bump, bump, bump, right to the bottom of the stairs. Alice's head would crack on the rock-hard flagstones. Ruby smiled, thinking, the bigger they are the harder they fall.

Was Ruby really planning to murder her much-loved twin sister?

Poor Blossom (sleeping innocently at the bottom of Ruby's bed) would get the blame. It would be assumed the young cat dashed up the stairs, silently, getting caught under Ruby's feet just as she passed the top of the stairs.

'Such a tragedy,' the neighbours would say, 'what an awful thing to happen.' The news would spread like wildfire: the whole village would be in a state of shock.

When the police and paramedics arrived, should she become hysterical? Maybe her eyes should be red and swollen. Yes, good idea. Once she'd made the phone call (sounding panic-stricken) a tiny drop of liquid soap, in the corner of each eye, would do the trick.

She'd already prepared her opening speech:

"How can I possibly live without her? I feel like part of me has died. I loved Ruby so much, we shared everything…"

However, falling in love with the same man – cheeky electrician, Dave Wallis – had brought nothing but misery and bad-tempered arguments.

They could share many things but not the love of a warm-blooded male.

Ruby crouched down beside the bannisters, ready to spring into action – it was pitch black. All she could hear was the tick of a grandfather clock and her sister's feet, stepping heavily across the threadbare landing carpet.

She shouted, '*Alice!*' as loud as she could, making her sister jump – then pushed her, with all her might, towards the bottom of the stairs.

Alice's scream was loud enough to wake the dead; her final words were a plea to her sister:

"Ruby, Ruby, for God's sake, help me…"

Ruby ran back into the bedroom shaking like a leaf. She put her hands (and then the pillow) over her ears, she didn't want to hear her sister's voice or imagine the unbearable pain she must be suffering.

She waited for twenty minutes before leaving the sanctuary of her bedroom. First things first. Ruby screwed a brand-new bulb in the table lamp and turned it on. When interviewed by the police she would curse the original bulb: its failure to illuminate the landing had been a major factor in the tragic death of her beloved sister...

Holding onto the banister rail (in order to steady herself) she peered down through the half-light. Her hands began to shake.

Alice lay there, (white-faced) at the bottom of the stairs. Her legs were sprawled out in a comical, unladylike manner, her eyes wide open but dead to the world. She looked like a stranger: a grossly over-weight middle-aged lady, dressed in a cheap cotton nightie...

Alice's head was resting on the bottom stair, a pool of blood had settled underneath her left ear. One of her eyes was swollen. Ruby checked Alice's carotid artery – no pulse, not a blip.

She gave a little shudder, a solitary tear rolled down her cheek, she brushed it away with the back of her hand.

"Alice's neck must be broken. I didn't really want her to die, I loved her. It was all Dave's fault. He played games with us, saying he couldn't decide which one of us he wanted to marry. He made a bad mistake, he should have proposed to me, not Alice."

There was something else she must do and it was just as important as changing the light bulb.

"Oh, blimey, the gold lockets! I must swap them over, immediately, before I forget."

Ruby climbed the stairs, her legs felt heavy, her energy levels were low. Each bedroom door had a nameplate attached by a small brass hook. Alice's name was surrounded by purple pansies, Ruby's by deep red roses.

"Oh, my God, this is a nightmare, what if I've overlooked something and get found out?"

She swallowed a couple of paracetamol tablets; her head was banging, she thought she might be sick. She must lie down on the bed before she keeled over. Perhaps she'd be able to sleep for a while. There was no rush to telephone for an ambulance, after all, when the 'accident' happened, she was fast asleep, she hadn't heard a thing…

Since the death of their parents, no-one (not even Celia) had been upstairs, so there was no need to change bedrooms, just swap over the nameplates! Besides, there would be no advantage as neither bedroom had been decorated since they were teenagers. The vivid yellow wallpaper, faded striped curtains and general ambiance were much the same in either room: jaded and utterly depressing.

From now on she must think like Alice, behave like Alice and talk like Alice. Not as easy as it might appear. Ruby would need to calm down, become less aggressive and smile more.

Would Dave be suspicious when he held her in his arms and kissed her, passionately?

She managed a weak smile, thinking, I've certainly got my work cut out...

Chapter 23

Celia Takes Charge

"Is there anyone we can call? Do you have a friend who'll come round and stay with you?"

Ruby was milking the situation for all it was worth. The ambulance had arrived quickly, no more than fifteen minutes after her phone call. She introduced herself by her 'new' name, Alice Lovegrove, then burst into floods of tears.

At one point she pretended to faint, it wasn't difficult, her nerves were in shreds. After a brief lie-down on the sofa and a hot cup of tea made by a good-looking paramedic, Ruby started to feel a lot better.

She was informed (in a kindly way) that the police surgeon had been telephoned and asked to attend the scene. It was necessary to confirm, legally, that her sister, *Ruby,* was indeed, dead.

Celia arrived at six-twenty. She tried to remain calm but inside she was feeling excited, nothing like this had ever happened before, not to her. Fancy being telephoned before anyone else! She couldn't wait to chat with the paramedics, they needed to know how capable she was; her friend would be in very good hands.

"No need to worry, I'll look after Alice, we've been friends for years. Such an awful thing to happen – the wretched light bulb had blown. Fancy that, on such a dark night. There was no moon either, jolly bad luck. I've had light bulbs for years, a few are covered in dust, well, the ones I can't reach. You take them for granted, don't you? That is, until they let you down!"

Celia smiled and nodded her head she was nearly out of breath. The paramedics, on realising Celia could 'talk for England', decided it would be a good time to leave…

"Oh, Alice, isn't it awful? Fancy little Blossom rushing upstairs in the dark, just as Ruby popped out to the loo – I suppose she wanted to sleep on a nice warm bed.

"It makes you wonder if there's been any other near misses, although I suppose the chances of that happening are a million to one. That bloody light bulb! Still, you have to admit – cats are rather silent creatures, aren't they?

"Oh, sorry, am I upsetting you? It's the shock, you see. I mustn't prattle on so. It's very early I know but would you like some breakfast?"

Ruby gave the impression she was thinking it over, when if truth be told, she was very hungry. The excitement had given her an appetite.

"Well, Celia, I suppose I could manage a couple of soft-boiled eggs, if it's no trouble, and a few slices of toast. I feel shattered, my muscles ache, I might have a shower afterwards, it'll help me relax."

Celia smiled and nodded her head.

"Yes, good idea, you do that, although we should eat something nourishing first – it's going to be a long day. I think I'll join you. I fancy a couple of eggs."

After the departure of Doctor Anthony Royce (the Police Surgeon) and the subsequent removal of the body, Ruby went upstairs for her shower.

Her head was spinning – *I'm Alice, I'm Alice* – the words went round and around until she felt like screaming…

Celia called out to Blossom, who, despite all the commotion, was still fast asleep on Ruby's bed. The cat stretched, arching her back, then wandered slowly down the stairs oblivious to the tragic accident.

Despite Celia having removed all visible bloodstains, Blossom stopped for a few moments to sniff inquisitively at the place where Alice had landed and cracked open her head. Had Blossom smelt blood on the cold, flagstone floor?

Celia opened a sachet of chicken and liver pate. She frowned: I do believe some cats have a better diet than many human beings…

"Oh, Alice, I simply can't believe Ruby's gone. The thought of walking into Temptations and seeing you there, all alone, well, it doesn't bear thinking about. How will you cope? I'm more than happy to help out in the shop until you find a replacement – but all that cooking, well, it would be too much for me – you know I've got a bad back. I don't know how you manage it, day after day. Perhaps you'd better close up for a few weeks, just 'til the dust settles.

"You mustn't worry about a thing – people will understand. Anyway, I'm sure Jim and Olivia will be happy to help."

Once the excitement had worn off, Celia returned home for a shower and a nap...

The following afternoon, Dave Wallis arrived, looking pale and visibly upset. He wasn't wearing his overalls, instead, he'd put on a pair of black trousers and a blue and white check shirt. Ruby thought how attractive he looked (how desirable) despite having dark circles under his eyes. He put his arms around Ruby, holding her close but saying nothing.

"Oh, Dave, I hope it wasn't something I said. What if *Ruby* was distracted, something on her mind? I know you said not to mention it but I did tell her about your proposal – please don't be angry with me, I couldn't help it, I was so excited."

Dave frowned. What the hell was Alice talking about, what proposal?

"Now look here, Alice, I made no proposal, let's get that straight. I know you had a few too many glasses of wine but blimey, that's no excuse! I'm fond of you and Ruby, maybe a little in love with both of you, but marriage? You must be joking. Anyway, you should know by now when I'm teasing you.

"Remember what I told you? I'm thinking of setting up in business of my own, that's more than enough to worry about. I'll have to take on a couple of apprentices, sort out the paperwork, go out and charm new clients.

"I can assure you, madam, I've no intention of marrying anyone, not now, not ever."

After Dave's departure, Ruby turned on the television, she neither knew nor cared what she was watching. Thundering hooves and clouds of dust – giraffes, zebras and wildebeest (all fleeing from danger) racing across the plains of South Africa. She understood their plight: they too were fighting for survival…

She looked at her watch, Celia would be coming round later; she wasn't sure if she could cope with her bossiness – not today.

What have I done? I murdered my twin sister but achieved nothing. I killed Alice because she told a lie, no more than that. If only I'd waited. I should have questioned Dave and found out the truth…

Jim was having coffee with Olivia, she'd opened a packet of chocolate Hobnobs, Jim's favourite biscuits. When they heard the doorbell, Olivia frowned – five shrill rings – the caller must have something extremely important to tell her.

Celia couldn't wait to tell them about the tragic accident. Naturally, she'd been called upon to take charge of the situation.

Every detail was picked-over: the wretched light-bulb, Blossom's night-time roving and the attractive features of one young paramedic.

She'd even boasted that her soft-boiled eggs had been cooked to perfection: a runny yolk, yet a firm white.

Once home Jim sat and thought about Celia's ramblings, what a shocking thing to happen, poor old Ruby. He poured himself a large whisky. He was fond of the Lovegrove sisters, they were immature but even so they brightened his day. If he so much as smiled at them, they blushed or giggled. He laughed. Did they want to have sex with him? Yes, of course they did! Didn't every middle-aged woman in Bridgeford and beyond feel the same way about him?

It hadn't occurred to Jim (not for one moment) that one sister had murdered the other or indeed, that this awful tragedy might be something other than a terrible accident. Of course not, why on earth would it?

He had an inkling that Dave Wallis (whom he'd spoken to once or twice) might be stringing the sisters along. When out for an evening's exercise (a gentle stroll around the village) he'd seen Dave bringing one of them home. Which one was he dating,

Ruby or Alice? Surely, Dave couldn't be romantically involved with both of them? Jim laughed, nice work if you can get it!

He shook his head, well, I wouldn't fancy them, far too fat for my liking, just a couple of sexually frustrated old maids. I don't know, they're nearly as bad as Celia. All three look at me with lust in their eyes, it must be something in the water!

The Lovegrove twins are identical, so how could Dave be sure which one was tucked up in his cosy bed? Perhaps he didn't really care, one thing's for sure, he must love big women. Oh, my goodness, I'd have been worried in case they broke the bed-springs!

Jim laughed at the very thought of it…

I'm lucky, I've got Shelly, she'll do for me. She's very pretty and so much fun. It's about time I contacted her. She must have stopped worrying about that idiot by now.

Jim looked relaxed. The fact he'd drugged and murdered Shelly's ex-husband was best forgotten, swept under the carpet. He preferred to put it to the back of his mind...

Chapter 24

A Disappointment for Jim

Temptations was closed…

Celia felt a great sense of relief, it wasn't optional, there was no point in soldiering on. Losing an identical twin under such dreadful circumstances could cause her good friend to have a nervous breakdown. Poor Alice, she must give herself time to absorb what had taken place.

Together, they'd written a brief notice and placed it in the shop window:

'Due to a tragic accident, Temptations will be closed for the foreseeable future. All enquiries, please, to: Ernest Boyle & Partners, Funeral Directors, 35B, Cheltenham Parade, Burford.

Tel: Burford 337744.

Jim decided this would be the perfect time to divulge the living arrangements and love-life of Celia's ex-husband, Alan Bamford. No doubt she'd be feeling fragile and emotionally drained.

He had intended to tell her the moment they returned home but Olivia insisted, no, definitely not, they must wait a while until they found the right words. There was no need to upset dear Alan and Bertie or embarrass Celia unnecessarily.

He didn't wish to appear callous, so he bowed to her better judgment. His day would come.

Alan Bamford was well aware his cover had been blown; he felt ashamed of himself. If he'd kept a cool head (instead of panicking) his new life with Bertie Fielding would have been acknowledged then soon forgotten. Even so, Alan and Bertie concluded there was something unnerving about Jim Foster, the man seemed to be revelling in their discomfort.

In their opinion, he was a man not to be trusted. One might go so far as to say, he was a troublemaker. He was too smooth, too perfect. A modern-day Casanova. On the other hand, Olivia had a kindly disposition: she would keep their secret.

When Alan spotted Jim carrying two suitcases out to the car, he'd acted on a whim and rushed to reception to find Olivia – it was now or never...

He'd looked uncomfortable as he handed over a small white card: it gave their names, address and the telephone number for The Hidden Tarn.

"Would you mind asking Celia to ring me? I'd be very grateful. She deserves an explanation. Poor woman, it's been nine years. Can we keep this between ourselves, please?"

"Yes, Alan, of course we can, please don't worry about a thing. I do understand your predicament. I'll have a quiet word with Celia. There's no need to say anything to Jim, he can be a little outspoken, even harsh, at times. It'll be better coming from me.

"Poor old Jim – he refuses to move with the times – he still sees everything in black and white."

Jim knocked on Celia's front door feeling full of confidence. I'll soon bring her down to earth, she won't know what's hit her! Celia asked him in, blissfully unaware of his reason for calling. It wasn't long before the penny dropped.

"Sorry to burst your bubble, Jim, but that's old news. Not long after your holiday in the lakes, Olivia came to see me and with great sensitivity, explained Alan and Bertie's love for one another. She managed to do so without gloating or being unkind – something you could never do.

"Now, if you don't mind, I have a pile of ironing to do. You can see yourself out."

Jim was livid. Olivia had deceived him.

How dare she do such a thing? It wasn't fair, it was his place to tell Celia, he had a right to see her fall apart...

Fancy sneaking behind his back, denying him the chance to see her reaction. Celia must have felt shocked and embarrassed. He scowled – no doubt Olivia was far too kind and made light of the whole situation.

Celia had yet to be punished for delving into his private life. He would never forgive her for mentioning Molly, Georgia de Vere or the fact he'd been charged with breaking and entering and punished accordingly. What gave her the right to judge him? She'd mocked him, belittled him and enjoyed doing so. No-one made a fool out of him and got away with it...

Celia rang Alan, feeling more than a little nervous. Whatever would they say to each other after nine years? A surprisingly warm and friendly conversation took place which gladdened both their hearts. She felt no animosity towards him. Perhaps, in the deepest, darkest corners of her mind, she had her suspicions; her husband must gay or bi-sexual.

Alan asked Celia if she would care to stay with them for a week or so – if she could bring herself to forgive him. He'd like her to meet Bertie, but only if she thought it was appropriate. The holiday would cost her nothing, it would be their treat. No date was set but she agreed, yes, it would be rather exciting to travel up by train...

Alan was surprised to hear of her move to Bridgeford-upon-Avon and delighted to know she'd inherited a stylish house in a most desirable area. He could remember, vaguely, her late uncle Reg, a shy man who preferred to stay out of the limelight. He'd met him just the once, at their wedding.

On three occasions, Alan had sent a cheque through the post (for a generous amount of money) but unfortunately, no letter had ever been enclosed. Was this yet another reason why she hadn't bothered to make changes to her will? Fortunately, an old acquaintance was living at Celia's previous address – he'd been diligent and forwarded Celia's mail straight to the Evesham Road…

The cheques had confirmed one thing – Alan was still in the land of the living – although whether she wanted him to inherit her house and all that went with it was a very different story.

Alan changed the subject. He appeared to be enjoying their conversation.

"Well, Celia, before I forget, we'll be travelling down to the Cotswolds quite soon, Bertie wants to visit his mum – she's in a nursing home on the outskirts of Banbury, a delightful place, it's called St Cuthbert's Court. She's very happy there. It's surrounded by wildflower meadows and her room overlooks a pretty little stream – it's idyllic. She swears she's seen a kingfisher, we're not sure, wishful thinking perhaps!"

Alan chuckled, making Celia smile.

She could tell (even though she couldn't see his face) he was happy and content in his new life. He sounded more out-going than before; even his voice seemed to have more authority.

"Mavis Fielding is such a happy soul. It'll be her 90th birthday in August, that's when we're planning to visit. She wants some binoculars for her birthday, so she can watch the birds. Apart from arthritis, she's marvellous. Could we pop in and see you? It would be no trouble making a de-tour."

Celia agreed to everything, in fact she'd be happy to see them, after all, they were, in a funny sort of way, her family.

Maybe one day she'd take a drive over to Banbury and meet Bertie's mum, she sounded like a wonderful old lady…

Chapter 25

A Careless Mistake

Ruby (accustomed now to being called Alice) re-opened Temptations for the two weeks leading up to Christmas. With Olivia working Mondays, Wednesdays and Fridays and Celia and Jim helping out on the days in between, it had been the right decision.

Sometimes, Ruby and Celia worked in the kitchen until ten o'clock at night. The extra-deep mince pies were extremely popular – there was a long list of orders to complete – they mustn't let anyone down!

Meanwhile, Jim Foster, enjoying the banter and light-hearted atmosphere, decided to dress up as Father Christmas.

One afternoon, a group of middle-aged ladies from Chipping Camden turned up (unannounced) in a dark blue Ford Transit van. Extra chairs were brought in and placed around the small tables in the rear of the shop. Their flirtatious behaviour suggested they'd visited a pub or two on the way.

A friend of a friend had mentioned the 'gorgeous hunk' working in Temptations, so a trip out was arranged. Deep-filled mince pies and lattes all round! The twelve cheeky ladies weren't disappointed, even a long white beard and crumpled red suit failed to quash Jim's sex appeal. The ladies refused to leave until they'd received a 'Christmas kiss' from Jim. He duly obliged...

After a short meeting (one Sunday afternoon) it was decided *Alice* should remain in the kitchen where her unique skills could be maximized.

Contrary to her original plans, Ruby decided against placing an advert in the shop window (or anywhere else) as things were working out so well. Besides, Karina, their Saturday girl, enjoyed working in Temptations and spent most of the school holidays behind the counter. She'd just started a college course (hoping to become a veterinary nurse) and needed the money...

Ruby was content. Her dear friends (already familiar with the local customers) were proving to be extremely popular behind the counter. However, although their cakes, pies and pastries might be acceptable at home, they certainly wouldn't reach the high standards achieved by the Lovegrove sisters.

Ruby missed her sister and guilt weighed heavily upon her shoulders but gradually, with their support, life returned to normal.

Over-hearing Jim as he charmed the ladies with his cheerful remarks and deep sexy laugh helped her through the day. Whenever she carried through warm pies, cakes or sweet pastries Jim was chatting to someone. The monthly takings had increased considerably, no doubt due entirely to her handsome new shop-assistant!

By the time spring arrived, Ruby was her old self again and even when Dave Wallis came into the shop, she was able to chat with him and keep calm. Neither of them felt uncomfortable and even when he called her Alice, it didn't cause her pain. Dave hadn't asked her out again and she was somewhat relieved. The romantic side of her life was over, perhaps she'd never fall in love again.

Dave Wallis (cheeky electrician) plus shy, unattractive identical twins, well, it was obvious to anyone – this unlikely friendship was destined to end in tears...

Celia was keen to learn and Ruby more than happy to pass on her cooking tips. On occasions she joined Ruby in the kitchen to decorate a few cupcakes or make the 'secret filling' for their ever-popular steak and ale pies.

Jim, Olivia and Celia seemed to be enjoying their new-found career. Never, in their wildest dreams had this mature, unlikely trio imagined themselves standing behind the counter in a village cake-shop. As they walked through the door of Temptations, they felt a buzz, a sense of camaraderie. Jim smiled, boyishly...

"Well, ladies, I think we should call ourselves the three amigos!"

Life was good, until the 5th of August when Ruby made a foolish mistake – she removed her beige cardigan…

The buzzer sounded: the meat pies, with their rich golden pastry, were cooked to perfection. The temperature in the kitchen was unbearable, twenty-seven degrees and rising. Ruby's cardigan was thrown, almost angrily, onto a kitchen chair. She sighed, poured herself a glass of home-made lemonade then added a few ice-cubes. She moved away from the fridge and sat down (or rather flopped down) on the nearest chair. Celia was sitting opposite, streaks of sweat visible now on her rosy cheeks. She opened the back door then fanned herself with the Daily Telegraph.

"Oh, sorry, love, whatever must you think? Same for you?" asked Ruby.

"Yeah, you bet," replied Celia, "I love your lemonade, so refreshing, not too sweet. Phew, it's like a bloody furnace in here!"

As her friend walked back to the fridge, Celia noticed something was wrong, very wrong. She could see (just below Alice's elbow) a rather unsightly scar. But that was impossible…

It was Ruby, not Alice, with a big scar on her elbow. It was Ruby who insisted on wearing long sleeves. It was Ruby who (as a teenager) cycled recklessly down a steep hill and crashed into a gravel driveway. Everyone knew it was Ruby…

The mottled scar had faded with time, but nevertheless, it was still red and unsightly.

Celia took a sideways glace, she was close enough to read the letter on the rose-gold locket. It was the letter A – of course it was – A for Alice, why wouldn't it be?

Celia decided to keep quiet, she was getting a headache, caused by the excessive heat. She glanced at her watch – it was a quarter past one.

"Alice, would it be okay if I went home now? Honestly, I've got a splitting headache, I need to have a lie-down. This heat doesn't agree with me…"

"Yes, love, course you can! You should've said, earlier. Don't come in tomorrow unless you're feeling one hundred per cent. We'll manage, Jim or Olivia will cover your shift. I'm so lucky, I'm spoilt for choice!"

Celia was glad she'd taken the car. Temptations was only a short walk from her home in the Evesham Road, but on a day like today, she would have struggled. It was humid, oppressive.

She stared at the darkening sky. Perhaps there'd be a thunderstorm later, if so, it would be most welcome. She nodded, yes, the rain cools things down and makes everything smell fresh…

After a drink of ice-cold milk and a couple of painkillers, her headache lessened. However, she was unable to relax. She stayed right where she was, in the chair by the living room window. There was nothing exciting to watch apart from Charles Greenwood trying to weed his front border with a large, unwieldy garden spade.

Celia shook her head. Oh dear, poor old Charles. If I didn't feel poorly, I'd nip over and persuade him to use a small garden fork or trowel. I'd better keep an eye on him, make sure he goes inside if the rain comes down...

After a cheese sandwich, Celia turned on the television, a romantic comedy was showing on BBC2, she'd seen it before but it didn't matter. It wasn't long before she fell asleep, not deeply, but enough to give her addled brain a rest...

Ruby picked up her bag and cardigan then set the alarm before locking the shop's heavy wooden door.

Within minutes she was safely inside her own home. She felt exhausted. She wondered (and not for the first time) how she would have coped without Celia, Olivia and Jim. It wasn't as if they were close friends (well, Celia, maybe) however, they'd all risen to the challenge!

It was their kindness and support that kept her going. She frowned. Oh dear, if they but knew what

I'd done, murdered poor Alice (pushed her down the steep wooden staircase) it would be a very different story. Still, there's no need worry, how could they possibly find out?

Perhaps she'd give Celia a ring, later on, see if she was feeling better.

She'd wait until after the six o'clock news, Celia might be taking a nap. Ruby returned from the kitchen, an orange-flavoured ice-lolly in her hand.

It was rather odd, Celia going off like that, she'd appeared flustered, although she'd been fine until they sat down together for a short break and a drink of delicious home-made lemonade.

She'd stopped for a moment and stared at Ruby as if she wanted to say something but at the last moment changed her mind. Instead, she'd frowned, shook her head then turned and walked quickly through the open shop door.

It was only then the penny dropped…

"Oh, my God," whispered Ruby, "what have I done? I've been such an idiot!"

She'd been so careless, it must have been the excessive heat, she knew full well she must never show her arms in public.

Had Celia noticed her scar? Was that the reason she fled? Was the headache no more than an excuse to get out of the shop? Celia would have been horrified. Fancy Ruby impersonating her dead sister – what a wicked thing to do!

Surely, knowing them so well, Celia was capable of working it out for herself. Dave Wallis had made up his mind (at last) and decided to marry Alice. After the tragic accident, Ruby saw the perfect opportunity to change her life: she grabbed it with both hands.

She would become Alice, marry her beloved Dave, and no-one (not even her new husband) would discover her heartless, deceitful plan…

Celia was getting excited. She looked at the kitchen clock, in two hours they'd be here, in her home! It was the 26th and very soon she'd be seeing Alan (after all these years) and meeting his partner, Bertie Fielding.

They were with Bertie's mum, right now, in St Cuthbert's Court, Banbury. Mavis Fielding, quite a character…

"Oh, Alan, you do look well. You've put on a few pounds – it really suits you!"

Alan was happy to give Celia a hug. Bertie moved towards her, she embraced him too, with warmth and acceptance, neither of them in the least embarrassed.

"Well, this is nice," said Alan.

"Isn't that what everybody says?" asked Celia, smiling warmly.

"No, we really mean it, Celia. We've been intending to get in touch for ages but you know how it is.

"Once Bertie left The Mayfair Hotel, in Knightsbridge, we started renovating The Hidden Tarn – complete re-fit from top to bottom. It's taken the best part of two years. We've done all the work ourselves, with a little help, saved ourselves a fortune. All we need now is some guests! Things are looking up, we've several bookings for September and October. Bertie was a head chef, you know, so he's in charge of all the cooking and ordering. We've taken on a waitress and a sous chef, so it's all systems go."

"Good for you, I'm sure you'll make a great success of your new venture.

"Do come through and sit at the dining room table. I'm afraid you're making me feel nervous, I've never cooked for a head chef! I hope you'll enjoy *my* cooking – chicken salad, followed by syllabub. Best to have a light meal if you've a long journey ahead."

"That's most thoughtful, Celia. Actually, we're spending tonight in Burford, another boutique hotel, The Red Fox. A chance to take a sneaky look at the opposition. It's surprising how many tips one can pick up.

"We'll set off early tomorrow, it's a fair old journey, two hundred and forty miles, just over four hours.

"By the way, can I have the recipe for that delicious syllabub? Our guests will love it!"

"Now then," said Alan, brightly, "we've been giving it some thought. How about coming to stay with us for your birthday? The first week in November. It'll be less busy for us so we'll have plenty of time to show you the local beauty spots and you can enjoy Bertie's cooking too! Well, what do you say?"

"Oh, thank you both, that's so kind. I can think of nothing I'd like more."

Chapter 26

A Cruel and Senseless Murder

"Jim, I'm really worried. I've telephoned Celia several times but I can't get a reply.

"I can see the bedroom light from here, it's still switched on even though it's mid-day. It was just the same yesterday but I didn't like to interfere. I don't think she's been closing the bedroom curtains either, I should have checked last night, when I went to bed…

"Alan and Bertie went to lunch the other day, I saw their car outside, you remember, that black Range Rover. Well, Celia must have been okay then, mustn't she? I rang Alice, she had to send Celia home the other day, she had a splitting headache due to the heat. Well, it was like a furnace in that kitchen. What if she's had a stroke?

"Something's not right, Jim. You know Celia, she's always up with the lark, gazing out of the window, scared she'll miss something! Perhaps her head's still bad, although she wouldn't leave the big light on, would she? Not if she was in bed feeling poorly. Shall we go over together?"

"Yes, good idea, I'm glad you rang. Give me five minutes, I'll be right with you."

Jim rang the front doorbell, several times, then, as there was no reply, they walked through the side gate and knocked on the back door.

Jim shook his head. No, she wasn't going to answer. He turned the door handle, the door swung open. Celia must have forgotten to lock it.

"Hello there, it's Jim!" he shouted. "Celia, are you upstairs?"

"Oh, my God, look over there!"

Olivia turned away, shielding her eyes.

A crumpled heap that had once been Celia Bamford lay motionless in front of the washing machine. She was deathly white and cold. A pool of dark, congealed blood surrounded her head. Olivia was in shock – she burst into tears.

"Come on, now, pull yourself together, this isn't the time to get emotional. Tears won't help her now. Whatever you do, don't touch anything.

"I'll ring the police. Go and sit in the living room, give me a shout when they arrive."

Olivia did as she was told. Despite the day being humid and the temperature already in the low twenties, she was shivering. The living room had signs of disturbance, a few drawers had been pulled out and thrown onto the floor. A black handbag had been left wide open. Olivia could see, without the need to move closer, Celia's distinctive red leather purse was missing. The dark blue Moorcroft vase was no longer in its rightful place.

Two police cars arrived – screeching to a halt...

"Jim, they're here!"

Jim rushed outside to greet them, guiding them inside through the back door. He explained to the sergeant exactly what they'd found on entering the property. He mentioned Olivia, pointing to where she was, in the living room, keeping well away from the disturbing scene in the kitchen.

As the uniform sergeant took a good look round inside and outside the property, the police constable joined Olivia with the intention of taking a statement. She could tell, immediately, the poor woman was in no position to give a clear and concise account of anything. There was only one thing to do, take Mrs Pendlebury home, make her a cup of tea and stay with her until she calmed down. Mrs Pendlebury's house, Broad-oaks, was just across the road, next-door to Gallica Rose, the beautiful 18th century cottage owned by the rather over-confident Mr Foster.

Olivia was more than happy to be escorted home. It would be a long time before the image of Celia's battered body (her poor face splattered with blood) faded from her memory...

P.C. Angie Woods had just completed her final six-week training course at the newly established Thames Valley Police college, situated on the outskirts of Reading. She'd been thrilled when her posting came through – the small, popular town of Burford plus surrounding villages. It was all she could have wished for; her parents were living no more than eight miles away, in Witney.

Angela Felicity Woods, was hoping for promotion – and sooner rather than later. The previous year she'd been awarded a first-class degree in Law and Politics.

After a cup of strong tea, Mrs Pendlebury began to open-up. She was prepared to talk about her neighbours and their private lives. It was obvious, Mrs Pendlebury was an empathetic lady who, under normal circumstances, would shy away from idle gossip.

Angie brought to mind one of her lecturers, Superintendent Melanie Savage; a particular phrase had stayed with her. 'Listen carefully, absorb every detail and try not to interrupt'.

Olivia shook her head then continued.

"This village is still in mourning. It wasn't long ago we lost Ruby Lovegrove, although that was a tragic accident.

"Are you familiar with the Lovegrove sisters who run Temptations, our wonderful little cake shop? They're rather eccentric but much appreciated. Jim, Celia and I have been helping out, we've thoroughly enjoyed it."

Angie nodded and smiled. Yes, of course she was aware of Temptations, who wasn't? Her parents drove over from Witney, regularly, to pick up a few delicious vegetarian quiches – they liked to keep some in the freezer.

Temptations was known to be the perfect pick-me-up after a long and difficult nightshift. Fantastic coffee and a selection of cakes or tasty pies to take home.

What a tragedy, she'd never heard anything like it. One night, Blossom, their beautiful little Siamese cat rushed upstairs in the dark, tripping up one of the twins as she nipped out to the loo. The poor lady fell down the stairs, cracked her head open and died from her injuries.

Being new to the village, Angie was aware of some details, but Olivia soon filled in the gaps. The light bulb on the landing had failed to work. Apparently, the dusty old bulb had been in situ for years. It must have been a terrible shock for Alice. Imagine waking up to find Ruby's dead body at the bottom of the stairs. She'd never get over it…

"Oh, it's okay, I'll answer it," said Angie, on hearing the doorbell, "it'll be the boss."

The first thing Olivia noticed about DCI Eddie Logan was his warm, friendly smile: unexpected and therefore very comforting under the circumstances. After he'd introduced himself, he asked if she was okay.

"Well, you know," she replied, shrugging her shoulders.

Angie made a cup of coffee for Eddie. When she returned, Olivia continued with her tale of woe.

"I nearly forgot to mention it, the village is still reeling over the mysterious disappearance of Lenny Barnes. Lenny hasn't been seen for nearly a year. His elderly mum, who lives in London, is in a terrible state. Shelly, his ex-wife, is my hairdresser, she's upset too. Lenny is, or rather was, the local estate agent. He'd no money worries, trouble with girlfriends or any reason to run away.

"Some people think this village is cursed: I don't believe in such nonsense. Nevertheless, a tragic accident, a disappearance and now, to top it all, we have a senseless murder. Poor Celia. Who on earth could do such an evil thing? It must be someone mentally deranged, someone high on drugs. They'd only stolen a couple of things – I   suppose they were after money."

DCI Logan looked across at Angie and nodded, she got the message.

"I'm sorry, Mrs Pendlebury," she said, "we really ought to be going. I'll give you a ring later, about six, just to make sure you're okay."

Later that afternoon, back at Burford Police Station, DCI Logan was on the look-out for Angie Woods. Eventually he found her, sitting in the canteen, alone. He smiled warmly then pulled up a chair.

"Okay if I join you?" he asked, clutching a mug of coffee.

Angie looked round the room and blushed. A few sniggers (barely disguised) could be heard in the background.

"Yes, of course, Sir, if you don't mind being the centre of attention. Oh, no, everyone's staring at us!"

Eddie sighed, why did people have to be so juvenile?

"Well, let's ignore them, shall we?

"Okay, Angie, I have a plan! I was most impressed by the way you behaved earlier today. I'm going to see Mr Foster tomorrow morning, about ten o'clock, so, if I square it with your sergeant – d'you want to come with me?"

Angie smiled shyly and nodded.

"You didn't think twice – you took Mrs Pendlebury home and stayed with her, keeping her away from that bloodbath. She was in shock. *You didn't ask – you just did it.* That's what the job's about – making snap decisions.

"I'm looking for a new TDC, must be female – our office is far too 'blokey' at times.

"Do you fancy a move to the CID? Temporary post at first – let's see how you shape up. It'll mean a year's CID course but it's a great career."

Eddie gave a cheeky smile.

"Nothing but long shifts, including weekends, prompting rows with your partner. You'll hardly ever see your family and friends. Am I tempting you? Some years, you'll work Christmas Day, Boxing Day and even New Year's Eve! Who wouldn't love being in the CID?"

He laughed and raised his eyebrows as if wearied by a heavy workload…

Eddie wasn't sure what to make of Jim Foster. On the surface, charm personified, but underneath? He sensed a man with inner demons. Jim loved being in the limelight but there was more to him than that – he appeared to crave adoration from every woman he met.

He hadn't been asked to contribute more than a statement regarding the previous day's events, nevertheless, Jim seemed determined to say his piece. The fact it was probably no more than a burglary that got way out of hand didn't seem to deter him in the least.

"Well, first of all we have Dave Wallis: something fishy going on there... Nice enough chap but no taste where women are concerned. Good grief, would you fancy getting into bed with the Lovegrove sisters?"

Jim laughed in a rather crude way.

"One at a time, I hasten to add! They're huge and not in the least attractive. I don't know what he sees in them. I assume you've met them?

"Oh, dear, I must stop saying 'them', after all, poor Ruby is no longer with us…

"You must add Dave Wallis to your list of suspects. If he fancies unattractive women, well, Celia certainly fits the bill. I assume you have a list?"

Eddie looked across at Angie, trying not to smirk. Jim Foster – why didn't he shut up? The man had far too much to say.

There was a brief lull when Jim handed round tea and biscuits. No cakes on offer. Once again, Temptations was closed for the foreseeable future…

"I assume you know Celia had a visit from her estranged husband and his gay lover, Bertie Fielding, just days before her death? Yes, very suspicious. That's yet another piece of the jigsaw.

"Are you aware (if my suspicions are correct) Alan Bamford and Bertie Fielding have taken part in a bigamous marriage? Well, that's something else you ought to sort out, and quickly, the law is the law…"

"Is it me?" whispered Angie, giggling, as they climbed back into the dark grey CID car.

"No, it isn't you. If we'd stayed any longer there might have been another murder!

"Mind you, the bigamous marriage will need to be investigated, although now that Celia is dead, the boys might not be committing an offense. I'll pass it over to someone who knows the ins and outs of the legal side of marriage – unless, of course, I choose to forget all about it...

"Now we have all the latest info on Alan and Bertie, I think we should take a trip up to the Lake District. We need to know why Alan Bamford suddenly decided to visit Celia after nine years. Interested? Do you fancy a trip? I'll speak to Sergeant Perkins he'll give you the okay."

"Well, Sir, I'll go with you on one condition. Can you assure me Alan and Bertie won't go on and on, like Jim *'know it all'* Foster?"

"Don't you worry," replied Eddie, giving his best steely gaze, "if they're too full of themselves, I'll soon shut them up!"

They were halfway up the M6 when Angie's phone rang, she grabbed it, eagerly.

"Hi, it's DS Hawkins. Hope Eddie isn't boring you rigid with his golfing exploits. If he mentions a hole-in-one, ignore him, he's lying…

"Now then, let's be serious. I've got some very interesting news for you. The boss is going love this – I kid you not – it's dynamite!

"I've just been talking to Celia Bamford's solicitor, a Mr George Wallingford, he's been giving me details of her will, it's fascinating stuff.

He's double-checked and much to my surprise, there's been no divorce. Now listen, this is the interesting part, even though they've been separated for nine years, Alan Bamford is still named as her next-of-kin and believe it or not, she's left him everything!

"Yeah, he gets the house in the Evesham Road, a decent sum of money in her Nationwide account and a few valuable investments too. Mr Wallingford said Celia's uncle Reg left her everything, he was very fond of her, she'd looked after him in his old age.

"Do you think Jim Foster could be right after all, Bertie and Alan planned to murder Celia, knowing Alan stood to gain a small fortune? Just think what they could do with the money. They had to act quickly, what if Celia changed her will? They'd lose everything!

"Maybe they got carried away with those renovations, borrowed too much money, in which case, now she's dead they can pay off their huge mortgage!"

"Wow, thanks, Sarge, there's plenty to think about, isn't there? I'll pass that on to the boss. Cheers then, we'll be in touch…"

From the moment she'd walked out of Celia's kitchen something had been niggling away in her brain; even now, she hadn't a clue what it was.

As Angie relaxed, enjoying the scenery, a thought popped into her head – oh, heck, her new blouse, the pink cotton one – she'd intended to wear it Saturday evening, she'd got a date.

Working with Eddie was so exciting it had completely slipped her mind. The blouse was still in the tumble dryer, damn, it would look like a piece of rag. She'd intended to give the blouse no more than twenty minutes, set on a cool temperature, iron it, then put it on a hanger to air.

Angie gasped. Something she'd been searching for had been prompted by thoughts of her creased blouse…

Yes, of course, the iron! Celia's iron was missing!

Celia's ironing board had been left out, in the kitchen, a blue and white stripy blouse laid across it. The sleeves were hanging down, looking pathetic, one ironed, the other crumpled. Surely, no-one puts the iron away when the job's half done, do they? You might be interrupted, turn it off, but then you'd finish ironing the garment before putting the iron back in the cupboard (or wherever else it lived) especially if only one item needed ironing…

Three clean mugs had been found on the draining board; washed and left to dry. Had all three been used by Celia or had she invited someone round? Maybe a friend turned up and she invited them in, right in the middle of ironing her blouse. Had Alan and Bertie returned, or was it somebody else? Someone closer to home?

She was pretty sure it wasn't Jim or Olivia, they'd have no reason to lie, unless one of them was the murderer which seemed highly unlikely.

What about Celia's close friend, Alice Lovegrove? Could she have been the mystery visitor? She must be so lonely without her twin sister. Whoever it was, they must have been the last person to see Celia alive…

Oh, thank goodness, Eddie was signalling left, he must be hungry too. In need of strong coffee and something to eat, he'd pulled up at the services. Angie gave a sigh of relief – she was bursting for the loo…

Sitting by the window, they discussed her theory, had there been a mystery visitor, maybe after dark?

"You're very observant, Angie, good work. I noticed the ironing board too, I had to squeeze past it to get to the body although the absence of an iron didn't register. The pathologist said the murder weapon was a blunt instrument: something the size of a house brick. Well, an iron is similar in size, albeit a very different shape. I imagine, with the aid of a handle, it would make a jolly good weapon.

"I expect Celia turned off the iron and made a cup of tea for herself and her mystery visitor…

"Well, anyway, Celia's 'guest' must have been there long enough for the iron to cool down, which is why there were no burns on her skin, only abrasions and a crushed skull…

"Ring Sergeant Perkins, please, right now. Celia's house must be searched again, we must find that iron. Thank goodness the wheelie bins won't be emptied until Friday.

"I'm sure the murderer wouldn't be stupid enough to hide the iron under the gardening stuff or recycling – not if it was covered with blood! No, they'd put it in the black bin, along with all the household rubbish, might even wrap it in something like a plastic bag.

If some junkie from the local area murdered her, he's not going to walk home carrying a blood-splattered iron, is he? I think, but I may be wrong, this crime was carried out on the spur of the moment, not premeditated. This person is an amateur. If I'm correct, that iron will supply us with fingerprints and DNA: not only from Celia but from the murderer as well...

"Jim and Olivia both said their downstairs curtains are never closed before ten o'clock. Being directly opposite, one of them would have noticed if a strange car was parked on Celia's driveway. You know what these villagers are like, they don't miss a blessed thing."

Angie laughed. "Well, Sir, if the murderer is someone local, we'd better go easy on Alan and Bertie, they may not be guilty of anything other than being utterly heartless towards Celia for nine long years…"

Before they left Burford Police Station, Eddie booked two single rooms. The Windermere Arms looked ideal, a pub with character, although it might be a bit noisy. Still, no matter, it was for one night only and after such a long journey Eddie would be capable of sleeping on a washing line…

After a decent bottle of wine, scampi and chips followed by a large slice of apple pie, they went to bed – alone. Eddie was a gentleman in every sense of the word.

Never, ever get emotionally involved with a colleague, it always ends in tears, he'd witnessed it on several occasions. Eddie was fifty-one, he was used to living alone. He didn't particularly enjoy it, but he was far too busy to join a dating agency or chase after pretty young women. If he settled down it would be with a more mature lady, not someone half his age…

Eddie had considered making this trip a surprise visit but changed his mind, there was no need to be callous.

Angie telephoned the boys the previous day, just before they left Bridgeford. It was only fair to let Alan Bamford know the reason for their long trek up here, to the Lakes. Poor bloke, he hadn't seen his estranged wife for years and now, after a brief reconciliation, she was dead, murdered.

When they arrived at The Hidden Tarn, the sun was already high in the sky, they shielded their eyes. Focussing on the dazzling water, without sunglasses, would have been impossible. This was Angie's first trip to the Lakes – she was more than impressed. She smiled at Eddie.

"This place is sheer perfection; the tarn, the white cottage, the spooky wind-blown trees, even the isolation – I've fallen in love with it!"

When Angie gazed at the purple topped mountains, she caught her breath…

If the boys were innocent (she assumed and hoped they were) she'd return one day, maybe with the man of her dreams…

Alan Bamford had asked TDC Woods (very politely) if they'd be kind enough to wait until after eleven o'clock. Breakfast would be over and guests would have left their rooms, giving them a degree of privacy.

Both men looked pale and shocked. After receiving such a devastating phone-call, it was hardly surprising. Suspicion must have fallen upon them, otherwise, why on earth would two detectives drive all the way up here? Any minor queries could be dealt with by the local police.

Angie was saying nothing, too busy taking notes on her laptop…

Alan decided to speak for the pair of them. They'd left Celia's house about four-thirty, after a surprisingly warm welcome and a delicious meal. They'd driven straight to Burford, taken their cases into the Red Fox and remained there until the following day.

Alan frowned, looking rattled.

"Before you ask, no, we couldn't have slipped out again without leaving our key, they insist on these things. Anyway, we'd have needed to walk through reception, there's only the one door."

"Oh, don't forget, we had room service – coffee and sandwiches sent to our room – about eight o'clock," said Bertie, interrupting.

"Well, that's it, really," added Alan, looking tired, "What more do you want to know?"

Bertie decided to pick up the story.

"The following day, after breakfast, we set off for home. We decided not to look round the shops. We're rather naughty at times, we get carried away, especially in the Cotswolds. Well, there's so much to buy!"

Angie laughed. She liked Bertie, a little camp and excitable but nevertheless, entertaining.

She stood up, ready to leave. Eddie looked across, shaking his head. Angie shrugged then sat down again which didn't look very professional.

"Well, before we go, I must ask you a few more questions. Do you have a mortgage on this property? It looks wonderful but the renovations must be costing you a fortune!"

Alan looked annoyed.

"Yes, of course we have a mortgage, a huge one…"

"Okay, thank you. We've been speaking to Celia's solicitor. I assume, during your visit, you were made aware you are *still* the sole beneficiary of her will? You get everything. The delightful house in the Evesham Road and several valuable investments. I must advise you to think very carefully before answering the following questions:

"You were married for, what, nine years? At what point during your marriage did you and Celia make a will? Have you made a new will recently or made changes to the original?"

Bertie hurried out of reception and towards the kitchen, he looked pale and anxious.

"I'll make some coffee," he whispered, looking over his shoulder...

Alan took a deep breath.

"Celia and I made our wills, together, during the first year of our marriage – which was, incidentally – no more than a sham. As you will have gathered, we were married for nine utterly depressing years.

"Bertie and I have been together now for several years and I can assure you, our relationship has been and still is – wonderful. Bertie contacted me, via Facebook, on his birthday, we call that day our special anniversary. We knew we were meant to be together, ever since we met at university, but, as the saying goes, *'life got in the way'*.

"Yes, of course I've made another will. I shall leave everything to Bertie. He's done the same for me.

"I would happily swear on the Holy Bible, Celia did *not* mention the subject and nothing was further from my mind. Please don't insult me by pretending you came up here to discuss anything other than that bloody will!

"Everything we did on or around 26th August can be checked out by you. We have receipts for the Red Fox hotel, Burford and for a full tank of diesel on our return journey. We filled up at the services on the M6. Even the visit to Bertie's mum in Banbury can be verified. We had to sign in and out of her care home, St Cuthbert's Court. I bought a box of Black Magic chocolates for Celia, in Bridgeford's new sweet shop, I paid by card, contactless. Let me assure you, each of these transactions can be confirmed by the time shown on my receipts.

"We have nothing to fear, DCI Logan, so please, as we're not under arrest, may I suggest you leave my property, right now?"

Back in the car, Angie stared at Eddie, she looked surprised and rather disappointed.

"Don't you think you were a bit harsh, Sir? You've upset them. They're very sensitive."

He shook his head.

"No, not really. Sometimes it's necessary. You have to stir the emotions, get people angry, that's when they trip themselves up. Anyway, I'm convinced – I'm sure you are too – Alan and Bertie have done nothing wrong, you could see it in their eyes. Either that or they're fantastic actors!

"I like to think I'm a good judge of character, you have to be in this job. Alan changed his will, leaving everything to Bertie. He assumed Celia would have written a new will too. Most women would have done so had they been deserted by their spouse.

"Well, Angie, where do we go from here? It's back to the drawing board, I'm afraid…"

Chapter 27

A Surprise Invitation

According to Eddie Logan's notes, Celia Bamford had more acquaintances than friends…

Eddie needed a little more background information. After a brutal murder, people had a tendency to remain tight-lipped, there was a reluctance to get involved. He was curious, did Bridgeford have any scary or quirky inhabitants? Who could be trusted to divulge the latest local scandal yet keep their mouth shut?

One lady (of similar age to Celia) sprang to mind. She'd certainly have her finger on the pulse. He'd telephone her, right now.

Eddie checked his watch, he was ten minutes early, Mrs Pendlebury wouldn't mind. She lived alone and might be looking forward to some company. No doubt the murder of poor Celia Bamford was going round and around in her head.

He hoped she wouldn't become hysterical or burst into tears; he wasn't used to dealing with highly emotional women…

"Ah, hello again, DCI Logan, do come through to the kitchen."

Eddie was almost speechless, had he come to the right house? His memory of Olivia must have become clouded. He'd seen her, just the once but her eyes had been pink and puffy through crying and she'd been shaking like a leaf.

Today, she was wearing a soft pink lipstick and lots of mascara. Her cheeks appeared flushed although that might have been caused by the heat of the oven. Eddie caught his breath, she looked beautiful, serene. Had she taken time with her appearance, just for him?

He sat at the kitchen table looking towards a rectangular lawn, neatly edged with numerous evergreen shrubs. He tried to look away but his eyes kept returning to her delicate features. He felt guilty: how he longed to take her upstairs and make love to her! He hadn't felt like this for years. It was the first time since the death of his wife that a woman had really appealed to him…

Oblivious to his amorous thoughts, Olivia busied herself with plates and saucepans. She turned on the kettle and looked at him, shyly.

"Although Guy, my husband, died four years ago, I still cook enough for two. It's a habit I can't seem to break. There's a fox who visits my garden every night, I enjoy spoiling him. I'm sure he's putting on weight!"

"Lucky old fox. You put me to shame. I've been on my own for many years but I've yet to cook a whole chicken. It's easy to get lazy and in this job, you never know what time you'll get home."

Olivia looked at him, flirtatiously.

"Do you have to be somewhere, like the police station? If not, would you think me rather pushy if I invited you to stay for a meal? It makes me feel miserable when I see just four roast potatoes, sitting there, next to the chicken.

"By the way, I have been told my gravy is second to none! I always add a little red wine, that's the secret…"

Eddie laughed and gave a warm, generous smile just as he had the first time they'd met, although, under very different circumstances.

"Okay, I give in! You've sold it to me. I'd be delighted to stay. What man, living alone could resist roast chicken? Thank you so much. Now, shall I open that bottle of wine?"

Olivia gave a sigh of relief; it was a long time since she'd seen a handsome man like Eddie Logan sitting at her kitchen table. She was going to enjoy this evening no matter what they discussed.

He'd said (on the phone) he needed her help but seemed in no hurry to bring up the subject of Celia's murder…

Eddie insisted on loading the dishwasher; as he did so he took surreptitious glances at Olivia. She must be seven or even ten years older than him but what the hell did that matter? She was gorgeous, elegant, well-spoken and amusing. Did she find him attractive? He could only hope and pray…

They sat next to each other on the sofa, watching a romantic comedy: the usual thing, two people meet, fall in love, then go their separate ways because of some silly mix-up. They get back together again (eventually) thus bringing tears to the viewers' eyes.

Olivia tried to top up his glass – he shook his head – no thanks. He rather wished she hadn't opened a second bottle. Olivia stretched then wriggled a little closer to him; she looked directly into his tawny-brown eyes.

"Wasn't that a sweet ending? I'm so glad they rekindled their love."

She giggled, girlishly, the wine making her feel relaxed and confident. With Eddie here, by her side, anything seemed possible…

Oh, Eddie, who says romance is dead?"

Eddie smiled warmly, but wasn't sure how to react; for some strange reason beautiful women made him feel nervous. Fear of rejection, perhaps. Was Olivia flirting with him? Yes, of course she was!

"I'll have to leave my car here tonight, in your driveway, if that's okay. I'll ring for a taxi. There's one thing I will never do – drink and drive. If caught, I'd lose my job and a damn good pension.

"Well, Olivia, it's time I asked you some work-related questions. To be honest, although you're distracting me (in a good way) I mustn't forget why I'm here. I need information, anything might help, so don't hold back. It's incredibly rare to come across a murder like this, an act of mindless violence, especially in such a peaceful village. I'm sure you're aware most murderers are known to the victim. Of one thing we can be sure, this murderer must have been high as a kite or mentally deranged."

Olivia looked thoughtful.

"To be honest, Eddie, we're all pretty normal, maybe a little boring. Some people think the

Lovegrove sisters are rather eccentric, I have   heard them referred to as 'creepy', but that's just silly and very mean. They liked to dress in identical clothing – like a couple of little girls – no harm in that. I'm sure they wouldn't hurt a fly. Poor Alice is all alone now, she must miss Ruby so much...

"Did you know there was only one way to tell them apart? Um. Ruby had a rather unsightly scar on her arm, beneath the elbow, she fell of her bike when she was young. They enjoyed teasing the customers, you know, pretending they were the other twin. People came to expect it, loved it and joined in the fun...

"Oh, I've just remembered something. I wonder if it's important? A couple of days before she was murdered, Celia rang me up, she sounded weird, frightened, she wasn't making any sense. I assumed it was something to do with Temptations. Anyway, she said she needed to speak to Alice, it was urgent. However, *she was dreading it,* what an odd thing to say! She was going to ring me back but she didn't, I'd forgotten all about it. Since her sister's death Alice has changed – she's more like Ruby now, more assertive. Funny, isn't it?

"Well, DCI Edward Logan, will any of that help with your enquiries?"

Eddie laughed and raised his eyebrows.

"Ah, I'll have to stop you there, madam! My given names are Edgar Robert – I try not to mention it – Edgar sounds so pompous. My father was Robert Edgar, after his father, well, I could live with that. Why the hell did my parents have to swap those names around?

"Changing the subject, somewhat, may I ask you something, erm, delicate? You and Jim Foster – are you an item? I don't want to tread on anyone's toes."

Olivia laughed and squeezed Eddie's hand.

"No, no, we're just friends, I promise. Jim's got a temper – sometimes he can be quite scary."

The taxi arrived. Eddie thanked her for the meal and a lovely evening. He smiled and confirmed that yes, her gravy *was* delicious. As they stood together at the front door, they became self-conscious, desperately wanting a hug but too shy to do anything about it. Eddie gave her a kiss on the cheek, that would do – for tonight…

Back home, brushing his teeth, he thought of Olivia – fancy calling me Edward – if only.

Still, it's easy to get someone's name wrong – at least I'm not an identical twin!

He tried to get back to sleep but it was impossible. His brain went round and around like a conveyor belt always ending up with the same thought, Olivia – she's absolutely perfect…

According to Olivia, Alice had become a lot more assertive since the tragic death of her beloved sister…

Why would she change? Was he making something out of nothing? Perhaps it had become necessary to 'toughen up' now she was all alone in the world…

A crazy thought popped into his head.

What if it was Alice who'd died and Ruby was no more than an imposter? Okay, but why?

Jim suggested Dave Wallis in connection with Celia's murder, in fact he'd been rather too keen to point the finger. Jim was a fool – Dave Wallis? How ridiculous – what possible motive could he have? Yes, Dave fancied a couple of middle-aged, unattractive ladies who weighed in at eighteen stone, but that certainly didn't make him a suspect!

Eddie tried to quash the idea that Jim might somehow be involved, it was highly unlikely but he couldn't rule it out.

He appeared to be getting nowhere fast…

Both ladies were madly in love with Dave; did he make a decision, finally, and Ruby refused to accept she would be the twin left all alone? The accident would have enabled Ruby to take Alice's place and no-one would ever find out. How convenient, how clever!

Oh my God, what if it wasn't an accident, what if Alice had been pushed down the stairs? He'd have to go to Temptations, speak with Ruby and ask her to roll up her sleeves. If she refused, he'd arrest her and take her to the police station. The weather had been hot and humid for over three weeks – who would willingly be wearing long sleeves in such conditions?

Poor, kindly Celia (who'd rushed in to help after the tragic accident) had been stuck in that stifling kitchen with the 'remaining' twin. According to Olivia, Celia had developed a bad headache, Alice sent her home so she could have a lie down. Was the headache due entirely to the oppressive heat or had Ruby been careless and bared her arms? If Celia discovered she was Ruby, not Alice, and confronted her, an almighty row would have taken place. Celia Bamford would need to be silenced – once and for all…

The enormity of the crime hit him. Was Ruby really capable of murdering her twin sister and then Celia? Yes, but what about the missing purse and the Moorcroft vase? Merely red herrings – she'd have nicked them and taken them home, trying to make it look as if a simple burglary had gone horribly wrong.

"Oh, hell," he whispered, "why do I do this bloody job? Perhaps I should have stayed on the farm with my parents. I prefer livestock to people..."

Eddie turned on the kettle and made a mug of strong coffee; it wasn't worth going back to bed. He picked up a couple of painkillers, he really needed them...

Back in the Evesham Road Jim was gazing out of the living room window, it was just after six-thirty: the prospect of yet another hot, sultry day loomed before him.

If only the promised thunderstorm would arrive and clear the oppressive atmosphere; it was starting to make everyone feel tetchy.

He frowned. A black Audi Q3 was parked in Olivia's driveway. It can't be Melissa, over from the States, Olivia would have told me if her daughter and family were planning to visit.

No-one has visitors this early in the day. Jim narrowed his eyes. Has someone been there all night? Not a man, surely? I don't believe it. I thought she was still in love with Guy, her late husband. I'll have to get to the bottom of this. I've always been the perfect gentleman but if Olivia wants sex, she only has to ask. She must know I'd be happy to move our relationship on to the next level. I'm an accomplished lover, I've never had any complaints…

Who the hell is he? Well, he won't be as attractive as me. You'd struggle to find another man in his sixties who looks this good! Jim did what he always did when feeling insecure: he gazed into the long hall mirror and nodded his head. Yes, thick grey hair, deep blue eyes, good teeth and a wonderful bone structure. I'm also highly intelligent.

"Yes, Jimbo, you've still got it!" He laughed in a rather creepy, unhealthy way…

Jim sat in the living room having his morning coffee. He was in a very bad mood. Where was he, this mystery man? It was time he went back to his own home.

A taxi pulled up: Jim could hear its distinctive diesel engine. A tall, good-looking man climbed out then handed over some money to the driver. He turned, smiled and waved as the taxi drove away.

Olivia opened the front door and rushed outside, a big smile lighting up her face.

The man bent forward and kissed her cheek. It was then and only then, Jim realised it was DCI Logan. He'd come to pick up his car.

Oh, thank goodness, at least he hasn't been there all night! Even so, something was going on, Logan must have been there the previous evening, drinking excessively, unable to drive home. Huh, he doesn't waste any time.

Pity he didn't drive home – if I'd seen him leaving Olivia's house, I'd have telephoned the police immediately. Anonymously, of course. How I'd love to drop him in it.

Jim sniggered, childishly.

"This is one enemy I won't be putting under the ground. Getting away with murder is easy, sometimes, but not when the victim is a high-ranking police officer!"

Chapter 28

The End of an Era

Many villagers (some in shock but nevertheless curious) stopped in order to peer through Temptations' large plate-glass window. There was nothing to see apart from rows of empty shelves, tables and chairs and an old broom, left standing in one corner. It was still closed, of course, no-one seemed prepared to take it on. Had their much-loved cake shop gone forever? The residents of Bridgeford missed the Lovegrove sisters – they'd been part of village life for well over twenty years.

One day, in the not-too-distant future, some enterprising person might rent the property and try their hand at supplying the villagers with apple turnovers, dark chocolate cheesecake, delicious meat pies and all the other tasty treats they'd so foolishly taken for granted.

Perhaps – but it would never be quite the same. Ruby and Alice, standing proudly behind the counter wearing their XXXL pink and white check tabards and pretty rose-gold lockets…

When DCI Logan arrived at Mulberry Cottage, all was quiet. He rang the doorbell, several times. Receiving no reply, he walked through the alleyway providing access to the rear of the properties. A small, paved courtyard was shared by three of the cottages. He knocked firmly, several times, then waited for someone to open the back door.

"She won't come to the door, lovey, I've tried, honest. She's hiding away from the world. Alice ain't been right in the head since poor Ruby died.

"Well, what do you expect? Them two was thick as thieves…"

Eddie smiled at the elderly lady who'd felt the need to join him outside the Lovegroves' back door. He produced his warrant card, she looked impressed.

"Oh, fancy that," she said, raising her eyebrows, "how exciting!"

"Would you mind standing back, please, madam? I'm going to kick the door in."

This he did with much gusto! After three kicks, the door sprang open...

Ruby was sitting in a rocking chair, half asleep, a large bag of sherbet lemons by her side. She stared at her visitors, a look of utter confusion clouding her face. A cheap cotton nightgown hung limply around her stout figure; after being dragged along the dusty flagstone floor for several days, the hem was filthy.

She'd tied a pink velvet ribbon around her greying hair – the very one she'd worn at primary school. In her hand was a photograph – Ruby and Alice, aged eight, playing in the sand on Brighton beach. Their chubby, smiling faces suggested they were having a good time.

The wood burning stove was alight even though the day was heavy and oppressive.

Ruby's neighbour (eighty-seven-year-old Violet Jamieson) followed Eddie through the door. He was very grateful. Would she like to make a mug of tea for Ruby? He was on edge, what would he do if the poor Lovegrove woman suddenly became hysterical?

Ruby looked at him in a quizzical way.

"I knew you'd come for me, Sir, I was waiting. I'm not a bad person but I had to kill Celia. Once she knew my secret, I had no choice.

"I couldn't pretend I was Alice, not after she'd seen the scar. It wasn't my fault, it was Dave's fault, he didn't want to marry either of us, he lied, he was only teasing us…

"When Alice said they were going to be married, I couldn't cope, I was jealous, so I pushed her down the stairs and all for nothing. Dave Wallis hadn't proposed, no, Alice made it up, cos she was drunk…"

Mrs Jamieson handed Ruby a mug of tea which she grabbed enthusiastically. A couple of slices of dry bread were put in the toaster. It was plain to see, Ruby hadn't showered or eaten anything nourishing for days.

"Now then, lovey, once you're nice and clean you can have some toast and marmalade."

With Mrs Jamieson's kindly words ringing in her ears, Ruby went upstairs for a shower. When she returned, she handed Eddie a bright orange Sainsbury's carrier bag.

"I expect you'll want this, Sir," she said, with no signs of embarrassment or fear.

Eddie glanced at the item inside the carrier bag but refrained from touching it. It was the murder weapon, an innocent looking steam-iron with Russell Hobbs, *Easyglide,* written on the side. Dark areas of congealed blood were still visible in several places.

"Mummy and Daddy will be cross with me, won't they? I threw Celia's purse and lovely vase into Mrs Clarkson's wheelie bin, well, she wouldn't mind, would she? She's ninety-seven and almost blind!"

Ruby started to giggle...

Eddie looked at Mrs Jamieson, shrugged his shoulders and thanked her for her kindness.

331

Ruby seemed to understand: she *must* accompany him to the police station and make a statement. They'd find her a suitable solicitor and he'd ensure TDC Angie Woods sat with Ruby when she was interviewed.

Chapter 29

An Unexpected Problem

Jim was restless. He'd read most of the Daily Telegraph and finished the cryptic crossword in record time.

Shelly Barnes rang, right out of the blue, he was delighted to hear her voice. She confessed to being lonely and in need of a hug (from an attractive, mature, gentleman) then laughed in a very suggestive way…

Jim smiled. Oh yes, that's me alright, bring it on. That sexy lady is just what I need – she's such a tonic!

Would he care to go round for a meal, tonight, about six o'clock?

"I'd be delighted, thank you, darling."

He checked his watch it was only two-thirty. Plenty of time to mow the lawn and trim the edges – if he got a move on.

He was delighted with his new ride-on mower, so quick and easy, mowing had become a labour of love. Lush green stripes, very impressive, even Charles Greenwood had peered over the fence and congratulated him...

"Ah, before I go outside, I'll see if I've got a reply to my email."

Jim had treated himself to a pure silk tie, burgundy and navy stripes, he'd ordered it from Harrods. It had a splendid, military look about it, the sort of tie favoured by male members of the royal family. Jim was becoming annoyed. It was ten days since he'd received an email promising the tie would be delivered the following day.

"One expects better from these people," he whispered.

"Oh, fancy that, a reply and an apology! That makes a change. There's been a distribution problem, huh, a likely tale. At least the tie has been dispatched."

'Please accept a £10 gift voucher (sent with your purchase) which may be used in conjunction with any future orders.'

An envelope had been pushed through the front door by Clint, the multi-tattooed postman. The letter was headed: Severn Trent Water Authority.

Dear Mr Foster,

A leaking sewage pipe has been discovered in your neighbour's garden; the property is owned by Mr Charles Greenwood. A camera has been used to survey all the pipes in the Evesham Road and several other faults have been detected. Much of the pipework is Victorian, ceramic and prone to cracking. Sometimes this can be resolved by inserting a 'sleeve' but on occasions the damaged pipework needs to be replaced.

At the rear of your property (Gallica Rose) tree roots have invaded the pipework – unfortunately, this means a great deal of work will be necessary. The repairs will be carried out at the expense of Severn Trent Water

Authority. We are hoping to commence work on or around the 14th of this month.

Any enquires: please telephone the above number between 9am and 5pm.

Yours sincerely,

George P. Metcalfe. B.Sc. (Hons)

Jim read the letter three times. It wasn't good news. What about Lenny Barnes' decaying body?

He'd built the rockery alongside Olivia's Cotswold stone wall; a shady spot amongst the fruit trees. He'd spend hours lugging those huge rocks around, digging over the soil, then building it up. Finally, he'd planted hundreds of spring bulbs.

What a nightmare, how could he prevent the water Authority from coming into his garden and causing mayhem? He could start by telephoning Mr George P. Metcalfe with his fancy Honours degree…

A young lady answered the extension number printed at the top of the letter.

"I'm awfully sorry, Mr Metcalfe is off sick at the moment, he has bronchitis. May I help you?"

She sounded pleasant enough, whoever she was. Perhaps he could lay on the charm, it usually worked, especially when conversing with a lady.

"Wait a moment, please, Mr Foster, if you give me the reference number, I'll get it up on the screen."

Jim explained that after the unexpected death of his beloved wife, Molly, and whilst suffering from acute depression, he'd moved to Bridgeford. Life in Eastbourne (so recently a dream come true for his wife) seemed pointless now, everywhere he went, all he could imagine was her beautiful face...

He stopped, as if overcome by emotion, then blew his nose, in a quiet, gentlemanly way.

"Do excuse me, my emotions are still raw; we were childhood sweethearts you see. I miss her so much...

"It took weeks to construct that rockery. I spent days planting hundreds of miniature spring bulbs, she

337

loved them so much. I've just ordered something online – you might laugh and think it's rather sentimental – a large piece of Welsh slate with 'Molly's Garden' engraved upon it. I'm so looking forward to getting it, it'll be the icing on the cake.

"Is there any way the pipework can be re-routed? Surely, it could be moved nearer the house, underneath the lawn, perhaps? I'm more than happy to pay for the extra work involved, you see, I'm rather frail now so unable to re-build the rockery. I've just had a nasty shock too – I've been diagnosed with terminal cancer…"

Jim surprised himself, where did that come from? He almost laughed. Nice touch, clever boy, yes, get the sympathy vote! He was really laying it on with a trowel – much more of this and the lovely Miss Abrahams would be in floods of tears!

"Oh, Mr Foster, I do apologise, our letter must have been a shock, it's the last thing you needed, especially when you've worked so hard on your project. Please leave it with me. I'll do my very, very best for you, I promise. Will you be okay, do you have any family nearby?"

"Sadly, no, I'm all alone. Thank you for listening to me, Miss Abrahams, I do hope you can sort things out for me. Goodbye, for now."

Jim laughed, another master class in acting. Sir Laurence Olivier would be proud of me...

Chapter 30

The End of the Line…

There was no way Jim could go round to Shelly's house, eat a meal and then be expected to make love to her…

He telephoned her the moment he'd finished cutting the lawn and trimming the edges.

He apologised. He was very sorry but he couldn't possibly see her this evening; he was feeling absolutely shattered. His sister (who lived in Sydney) had just died, from a massive heart attack, she was ten years younger than him. He needed to be on his own. Shelly was very understanding.

"Oh Jim, that's dreadful. Please let me know if I can do anything to support you. Ring me when you feel up to it. Take care, sweetheart."

The days were ticking by. It was the 9th yet not a word from Miss Abrahams. What should he do, chase her up? There was no way he could dig up Lenny's body and get rid of it. Charles Greenwood or

Olivia might be watching him from their respective bedroom windows!

Burying Lenny had been easy, a doddle. Olivia had been in hospital and Charles couldn't tell the difference between an effigy and a deeply frozen body. A few quid's worth of fireworks and several sausage-rolls later, poor old Charles had turned into a ten-year-old schoolboy – happy as a lark…

The mere thought of a leaking drainage system made Jim feel panicky. On the surface he was the life and soul of any party but sometimes life scared him, as it did now, when he wasn't in control.

During a sleepless night Jim made an uncharacteristic and totally unnecessary decision, one that would prove to be the biggest mistake of his life…

The following morning, he felt calmer – all good things must come to an end.

He looked in the fridge, oh, no, bacon and eggs, I wouldn't be able to keep it down.

"The condemned man refused to eat a hearty meal," he whispered, but failed to laugh at his own joke.

The single sock was removed from the back of the airing cupboard. The foil strip, containing seven Oxycodone capsules was still there, waiting...

Jim filled his fountain pen with turquoise ink – it had been designed in the 1920s – a rare and beautiful pen. This Parker Duofold, complete with solid gold nib, had been the pride and joy of his late, domineering, father.

'DCI Logan' was written on an envelope in Jim's stylish hand-writing.

Sir,

By the time you read this I will be long-gone...

However, as Eddie would soon find out, Jim's carefully chosen words were more of a list than a straight-forward letter:

1: My wife did not die from natural causes, as stated on her death certificate. I killed her by placing a pillow over her face. It was very quick, she didn't suffer. I had no choice, she was preventing me from marrying the woman of my dreams, Georgia de Vere. Sadly, my carefully crafted plans came to nothing.

2: Bernie P Epstein had been a good friend for many years – until he double-crossed me. His unsolved murder has been a thorn in the side of the Metropolitan police; they need worry no more. Murder is easy, if you speak to the right people. It isn't cheap but anything can be bought, if you're prepared to pay the price...

3: Poor Lenny Barnes – he thought it was acceptable to blackmail me! He mocked me (I won't go into the details) and disapproved of my relationship with his ex-wife, Shelly Barnes. I put three Oxycodone capsules into his drink, which sent him to sleep, then suffocated him with a plastic bag – as easy as pie.

After my death and subsequent burial, you might care to dig over my lovely new rockery. I'm aware 'six feet under' is the required depth, however, you will find Lenny is a little closer to the surface...

My will (all legal and above board) can be found in the top right-hand drawer of my desk.

You may donate my fountain pen to Scotland Yard's 'Black Museum' which I've heard is fascinating. It will lend a touch of class.

Please don't think too badly of me. Perhaps I possess the courage to do the things cowards can only dream of...

Regards

James W Foster.

Clint, the postman, was holding a square-shaped cardboard box and a long white envelope. When he shook the box, gently, he could imagine the golf balls circling round inside. He chuckled, Mr Foster said he'd ordered a dozen, he couldn't resist, they were half price. Titleist too, a very good make, apparently. Clint wasn't a golfer he preferred a game of football with his mates or a long walk with his wife and five kids. He peered through Jim's living room window. The car was in the drive but where was Mr Foster? He checked his watch – eleven-thirty. Maybe he was in the shower or the rear garden. Clint rarely gave up, he hated leaving parcels on doorsteps.

Despite the sound of the doorbell's urgent tone, Jim remained where he was, fast asleep (apparently) in a pale leather armchair – an empty glass by his side. Clint peered through the front window, he started to panic – something was wrong, very wrong. Jim's body had slumped forward as if ready to fall out of the chair and onto the floor. Clint knocked on the window, Jim didn't move an inch. Mr Foster would never be drunk at this time of day! He'd better ring 999 and wait until the police and ambulance arrived.

DCI Logan was instructed to attend the scene – a 'sudden death' needed to be handled with expertise.

Clint looked pale and upset when he put Mr Foster's letter and parcel on the kitchen table.

Eddie noticed a foil strip with Oxycodone written on one side.

There was another letter but this one made him catch his breath – it had *DCI Logan* written on it…

After reading Jim's confession, Eddie was in shock – he had to sit down. It was awkward, he couldn't breathe a word to Clint even though he seemed to be a decent, trustworthy sort of chap.

Eddie ripped open the second white envelope, assuming it to be nothing of any importance. It was Jim's long-awaited reply from Severn Trent Water Authority (written by Miss Abrahams) it had a friendly, empathetic tone.

She was pleased to inform him that Mr Metcalfe had recovered quickly from his bout of bronchitis and was back in the office. He was in the process of re-working the plans for new sewage pipes, not only for Jim's rear garden but also for the gardens of his immediate neighbours, Mr. C. Greenwood and Mrs. O. Pendlebury.

'With a little bit of repositioning and imagination, your lovely new rockery need not be disturbed after all, although a great deal of your lawn may need re-seeding. The work will be postponed for a couple of weeks, to allow new plans to be finalised. We

regret to inform you a charge of £1,750 will be made to cover some of the additional work involved.'

Clint continued with his round, but he was feeling out of sorts. Melanie Monroe (further along the Evesham Road) took him inside and gave him a cup of tea and two custard creams. Melanie was a lonely lady who'd once been a very successful actress; despite being in her early eighties she still wore false eyelashes and rather too much make-up.

Clint was happy to sit down and talk…

"Honestly Mel, it was such a shock. I really liked Mr Foster he was great! We had a sort of friendship, you know, he liked a bit of banter. He always opened his front door if he saw me walking up the drive. Why on earth would he commit suicide? He had so much to live for. You don't think he was ill do you, something he couldn't face? I saw that empty strip of Oxycodone capsules – I wonder if he took all ten? My mum took 'em for a slipped disc, ever so strong, they are! I shall miss him; mind you, so will half the middle-aged ladies in Bridgeford!"

Melanie smirked.

"Oh, Clint, you are awful! Yes, he was a very good-looking man. He reminded me of a few actors I used to know. Suave, sophisticated, you know the type. I'll tell you something, Jim would have been welcome in my bed – any day of the week!"

Clint chuckled, thinking, sorry love, no chance – not at your age...

Melanie nodded her head.

"You could be right, he may have been ill, too proud or too scared to talk about it. I'm sure you're aware he was thick as thieves with that Pendlebury woman, they went on holiday together, up to the Lakes. She'd know if he was ill.

"Well, young man, do let me know if you hear anything."

Chapter 31

Ruby Settles In

A large black woman sidled up to Ruby. Her hair was thick, frizzy and decorated with red and blonde streaks. Her eyes were big and beautiful. She peered at Ruby over a pair of red-framed spectacles, then smiled, warmly.

"You're new, aren't you? What's the problem, babe?" she asked, sitting down opposite Ruby.

Ruby was absolutely terrified: what the hell was she doing in this madhouse, on remand, charged with murdering her beloved sister and her good friend Celia Bamford?

"It's alright, honey, you can talk to me – I've been in here eight years – there's very little I haven't heard before."

Desiree Yusuf (originally from Nigeria) listened intently as Ruby poured her heart out.

"I didn't want to kill Alice, I loved her, but I couldn't let her marry Dave Wallis. It wasn't fair, he was leading us on – he had no intention of marrying either of us. Celia Bamford was our very best friend. We always had a good laugh when she came into the shop. We used to eye-up all the men, see who we fancied. They were good times. Oh my God, what have I done?

"When Celia noticed the big scar on my arm, she knew immediately, I wasn't Alice. The game was up, I'd been found out. I went round to Celia's house, one evening, after dark. She asked me in. The ironing board was still out, although the iron was cold, she'd stopped for a cuppa. Well, I grabbed it and hit Celia around the head, several times, as hard as I could. It was horrible, she fell to the floor, dead. I put the iron in a Sainsbury's carrier bag and walked home, slowly, so I didn't stand out.

I'll tell you something, Desiree, I didn't even care when that handsome policeman turned up, no, I've never felt so miserable in my life. When you're an identical twin, you can't cope on your own…"

"You bloody fool," said Desiree, scowling, "why the hell didn't you kill that bastard, Dave Wallis? It was all his fault, by the sound of it.

"Never mind, girl, you'll be okay in here. Sisters gotta stick together."

After witnessing her tears and sensing her distress, a few other women joined Ruby as she sat waiting to begin her art class. A youngish girl, who'd murdered her abusive partner, asked Ruby if she had any fags.

"No, sorry, I don't smoke," she replied, looking guilty.

The women listened, fascinated, as Ruby described the delicious cakes, pastries and meat pies made by her and Alice in their very own artisan cake shop.

"What the hell does artisan mean?" enquired Butch, a solid-looking lady with numerous tattoos, large biceps and cropped, bleached hair...

"It means you've made everything yourself. I suppose it also means posh," replied Ruby, nodding her head.

"Yes, it definitely means posh. You can charge a lot more for stuff like dark chocolate cheesecake. Do you know, you could get sixteen slices out of our largest cheesecakes, yeah, at three-ninety-five per slice – *we made a massive profit!*"

The ladies smiled, looked impressed then congratulated her for being so clever with money.

One skinny young girl, with spots and pimples, sighed.

"Cor, wish I'd been born somewhere like that, a classy place in the country. I've always lived in Peckham, in a poky high-rise flat. Do you know something? I don't think my mum made a cake in her life – too busy smoking weed.

"Here Rubes, I've had an idea! You said you're gonna plead guilty, right? Let's say you get twenty years. If you behave yourself, you might get out after fifteen years, some folks do. You can get another cake shop, we'll come and work for you!

"Oh, babe, I can't wait to try them steak and ale pies."

The ladies laughed, punched the air then patted Ruby on the back. Ruby was feeling better by the minute.

If the Governor agreed to her request (a move to the prison kitchens) she'd feel able to cope, he might even appreciate her expertise, after all, once she'd been sentenced, he would be seeing a lot more of her!

Would life be so very different? She'd be doing what she loved, cooking, but on a far greater scale. Huge saucepans filled with her very own vegetable soup. She'd be cutting slices of blueberry and apple pie, not for a few regular customers but for hundreds of ladies – she'd be very popular.

Besides, she wouldn't be thinking of Alice and Celia, continuously. So many dark thoughts, so much guilt...

At last, Ruby felt able to relax. If she earned their trust and was accepted, she might have a reasonably bright future. She'd meet lots of new people (although some of the women looked very scary) and have more friends than she'd had at home.

"Ladies, I've got an idea! How can I persuade the Governor, that stupid old fool, Horace Smythe, to let me have a few cases of ale? I'll need some for my steak and ale pies. I know – I'll get him to order too much, we'll hide a few bottles, then we can have a party."

The ladies cheered. Ruby Lovegrove was okay – better than okay – she'd soon fit in…

Chapter 32

Made for Each Other

The unexpected suicide of Jim Foster was turning out to be more than a little complicated; the reason being, it was totally out of character.

Eddie had spoken to Jim at great length (after Celia's murder) but that didn't help him at all. He didn't seem the type – was there a 'type'? Where emotions were concerned, nothing surprised Eddie. He'd seen it all before: love, hate, greed, jealousy – all these emotions make people behave irrationally…

First things first, he'd have a word with Miss Abrahams, from Severn Trent Water, her letter had been extremely empathetic but arrived too late.

"Oh, yes, I remember Mr Foster. Such a sweet man, how very sad, I didn't realise he was *that* ill. I promised I'd do everything in my power to get the drains re-directed. They would have ploughed right through his memorial rockery – I couldn't have that. He'd spent days turning it into something special. To make matters worse, he'd just been diagnosed with

355

terminal cancer, well, I felt duty-bound to support him. I was hoping to go and visit him, one day this week. He hadn't got any family. No, only a sister and two nephews in Sydney, Australia.

"I knew Mr Metcalfe would sort things out, he's a good man. He worked his socks off, sorting out a new route for Mr Foster's drains and those of his neighbours – they have to join up, of course. Anyway, I wrote and told Mr Foster the good news, I assume he received my letter? I do hope it gave him a little comfort before he passed away."

Eddie decided not to inform Miss Abrahams that Jim's death was suicide, why burden her? Once the lurid details of Jim's evil past hit the tabloid newspapers, she'd soon find out!

At last, things were beginning to make sense. Jim must have been panic stricken. What if the rockery was dismantled, then dug up in order to lay new trenches? Lenny's decaying body would be discovered. Jim was backed into a corner, there was no escape.

Was Jim terminally ill? Was that the other reason he'd taken his own life? Eddie shook his head. This was by far the most complicated case he'd had to deal with. Three murders, yet Jim would never be punished. Who said getting away with murder was easy? It was – for Jim Foster.

If the drains in the Evesham Road hadn't been old and leaking, Jim's life would have been perfect...

He must speak to Jim's doctor: he didn't relish the idea; doctors were reluctant to divulge or discuss their patients' illnesses. Still, it might be okay if the patient is deceased. Where did the Oxycodone capsules come from? He'd heard of them – very strong and no doubt addictive. They weren't something bought over the counter in Boots, no, they had to be prescribed by a doctor.

Perhaps he'd have a word with Olivia before he telephoned the surgery.

He smiled, any excuse. He'd fallen for her, there was no point denying it.

He longed to make love to her – he could think of little else…

Olivia would know if Jim was suffering from cancer. If he confided in anyone, it would have been her.

She opened the front door, a smile lighting up her beautiful features.

"Oh, how wonderful, I hoped it was you. Come through, I'm in the kitchen, as usual."

Olivia gazed into his eyes and blushed. She turned away, feeling embarrassed by her amorous thoughts and her sudden desire for sex.

After Guy passed away (so unexpectedly) she thought she'd be spending the rest of her life alone, yet here he was, the handsome man she'd fallen in love with, standing right in front of her. She longed to grab him by the hand and lead him upstairs to her bedroom. Would he be surprised? Unlikely. I may be sixty-one but when I'm with Eddie, I feel more like twenty-one.

She hoped Eddie felt the same way about her. She didn't know, or even care if there was a woman in his life. There was just one problem, she'd lied (or rather hadn't corrected him) when he guessed she was, *'About fifty-five?'* Would he still fancy her if he knew her true age?

"Is this work or a social call? It's hard to tell when you don't wear a uniform. Oh, Eddie, I do like a man in a uniform!"

She winked at him in a rather provocative manner. Eddie laughed.

"Sorry, Olivia, that particular ship has sailed, you'll have to use your imagination. If you see me wearing a uniform, be prepared for a shock, it'll mean I've done something very wrong. I've no intention of leaving the CID, ever, it's my life.

"You could say this is work and pleasure; once again, dear lady, I need your help.

"Oh, hang on a minute, something's cooking, it smells delicious. The last time I came to see you I was invited to stay for a meal – not that I'm hinting…"

Olivia said not a word: instead, she picked up another dinner plate, put it on the kitchen table, walked towards him and kissed him on the cheek. Eddie responded by giving her a hug.

"Right then, just a few important questions about Jim Foster. Did he tell you he had terminal cancer? You saw him frequently, did he appear ill, or in pain?"

Olivia raised her eyebrows. Jim, ill? Surely not. He hadn't said anything. He always seemed remarkably fit for a man who wasn't far off seventy. When they'd stayed with Alan and Bertie, Jim had scampered down the slope towards the hidden tarn (wearing Wellington boots) showing no signs of breathlessness or fatigue.

A few days after she'd returned from hospital, he'd asked her to pop round and have a look at his new rockery. Piles of soil had been arranged into a small hillock, then huge rocks had been strategically placed on top of it. He'd done all the heavy work himself then planted hundreds of spring bulbs:

crocuses, miniature narcissus, snowdrops and cyclamen. A splash of colour in memory of his beloved wife, Molly. All that bending – in her opinion Jim Foster was fitter than most men half his age.

"The thing is, Eddie, sometimes people have a little niggle but they're too scared to go and see the doctor, aren't they?"

Eddie smiled, briefly, but his expression soon changed. He stared out of the window into the far distance. He couldn't talk about his wife, not yet, not to strangers – he still missed her and thought about her every single day.

Helen had discovered a lump in her right breast but she wasn't unduly concerned, after all she was only thirty-eight. She'd convinced herself it was only a cyst, after all they were relatively common, weren't they? The months went by and eventually she mentioned it to Eddie. They went to see the specialist together – but it was too late. She died eighteen months later…

"Is everything okay, Eddie? Have I said something to upset you?"

"No, I'm fine. One day, Olivia, I'll tell you all about it…"

The following morning when Eddie telephoned Doctor Gupta, he was in for a few surprises. The GP (who'd been checking through Jim's medical records) told Eddie Mr Foster had *never* seen a doctor or specialist regarding any serious ailments; not recently or in the past. Apart from a yearly flu jab, Mr Foster had been a stranger to the surgery and one could almost say – the whole medical profession! Doctor Gupta chuckled in a light-hearted and friendly way. Eddie thanked him for his help, but nevertheless, frowned.

How bizarre. Why on earth would anyone say they were terminally ill when they weren't? Sympathy? Yes, that was one reason. Foster was a clever, devious chap. Severn Trent would feel obliged to show a little compassion and if at all possible, give way on the drains. Poor Mr Foster, they'd say, he's going through a rough patch and may not have long to live. Some kindly person might suggest diverting the drains, after all, it could turn out to be cheaper as a long-term solution.

If Jim could charm Miss Abrahams, maybe he could put pressure on her, convince her to get her boss to steer the plans well away from the rockery and therefore, Lenny Barnes' decaying body. It was worth a try.

If only he'd waited a little longer for her letter to arrive...

Chapter 33

So Many Questions...

Olivia sipped her coffee in a genteel and ladylike fashion...

She'd given herself a tension headache, (hardly surprising) she couldn't stop thinking about those wretched Oxycodone capsules. Jim must have found them in Charles Greenwood's house, probably in the kitchen. Did he discover them on the very day they'd visited Charles, together?

He must have put them straight into his jacket pocket, how odd. Why on earth would Jim steal them and take them home? They'd searched high and low for the damn things, why didn't he say he'd found them?

Had Jim decided (even before they went round to see Charles) to drug and murder Lenny Barnes? Maybe, but how could he possibly know the capsules would be there?

Oh my God! The pineapple, the capsules and the tea-towel – the whole episode had been no more than a farce. An elaborate ploy – acted out by three people – with Jim pulling all the strings.

Olivia caught her breath – her hands were shaking – she poured herself a glass of dry white wine. Looking up at the kitchen clock, she smiled ironically, it was only nine-fifteen.

"I definitely wouldn't recommend dry white wine for breakfast, no, it tastes pretty foul after a couple of Weetabix!"

Olivia felt sick inside. How dare he behave in such a cruel and heartless way! Jim had convinced poor Charles that he'd watched him enter her kitchen via the backdoor (when she was mowing the lawn) then walk out again carrying these three items. She hadn't given it a second thought, until today.

It had been Jim, not Charles, creeping around searching avidly for her powerful painkillers…

Charles had been devastated, he couldn't recall doing such a thing, in fact he'd burst into tears. He'd been used as the 'fall guy.' Jim was happy to trick a man with Dementia – he had no scruples at all.

According to Jim's confession, Lenny had been given three Oxycodone capsules (to knock him out) leaving seven in the foil strip. The capsules had been prescribed for her – and her alone – by Doctor Gupta.

Eddie had revealed aspects of Jim's past life that were so bad, so heartless, she had to promise never to repeat them to a living soul. He trusted her, she wasn't a gossip – besides, who could she share a confidence with? Alice and Celia had been murdered and Ruby was in prison.

Olivia and Jim had been close friends although not romantically linked. They'd been on holiday together, visited local restaurants and enjoyed walking in the beautiful Cotswold countryside.

They'd even considered 'sharing' a small dog. The whole ghastly situation left Olivia shaken and fatigued…

Olivia knew she must speak to Eddie – she had to tell him the truth…

Jim had been aware she was taking strong painkillers she'd mentioned the side-effects more than once. Jim stole them – he had no choice – it was the only way to get his hands on a strip of 'prescription only' medicine.

It was only vanity holding her back.

"Grow up, girl," she whispered.

Taking these strong painkillers wasn't the problem, she certainly hadn't become addicted to them. It was the *reason* for taking them that make her feel awkward – she would need to tell Eddie she'd been waiting ages for a hip-replacement. It would be okay if they were the same age, but the mere suggestion of a hip-replacement suggested someone old and decrepit – in her eyes.

Later that day she received a call from TDC Angie Woods, a minor matter regarding Jim's next-of-kin in Australia. Did she have a phone number? She didn't…

Olivia grasped the nettle – it was now or never. When she told Angie of her fears, the young detective burst out laughing.

"Oh, Mrs Pendlebury, let me assure you, you need have no worries on that count. The boss is crazy about you. He talks of little else! Only the other day I said, Sir, for goodness-sake, go and tell her, quickly, before you chicken out."

Olivia breathed a sigh of relief. She sat in front of the patio doors counting the goldfinches, there were eleven, impressive. She was half-asleep when the phone rang.

"Hi there, it's me, Angie – again. I've got to tell you this, it'll make you smile, I promise!

"One of our detective sergeants is off sick, arthritis, she's awaiting a hip-replacement and guess what, she's only forty-one. Hope that makes you feel a whole lot better. Anyway, age is just a number. Don't worry, Mrs Pendlebury, I shall get you and Eddie together if it's the last thing I do!"

"Bless you, Angie, or should I call you cupid?"

Eddie rang the doorbell, breathing deeply, was he about to make a complete fool of himself? Had Angie been winding him up? Olivia could see him clearly through the frosted glass panel, she ran down the hallway like a young girl. In her haste to reach the front door, she almost tripped over the edge of a pastel-coloured Oriental rug. Eddie was grinning like a Cheshire cat.

"A certain young detective – who shall remain nameless – said I must visit you. I was instructed to begin the courting process!"

"How honest of you to tell me, although I have heard more romantic statements. Um, fancy coming inside?"

He handed her a bunch of pale pink roses, she laid them down gently on the small oak table. Eddie smiled in a cheeky, boyish way.

"By the way, they're definitely not Gallica roses – I checked with the florist – they're hybrid tea roses, so much nicer."

From the moment she'd set eyes on him, Olivia had been longing for this moment...

"Come here, Eddie Logan, I want you so much. Please don't say a word, just hold me..."

They fell into each other's arms. Eddie sighed with relief; thank goodness she felt the same way about him. Their first kiss seemed to last for an eternity, neither one wishing to break away...

The following morning, they gazed at each other over the kitchen table, this was the first day of the rest of their lives...

Neither of them felt in the least embarrassed by their passionate encounter. Eddie was the first to speak.

"You know I'm in love with you, don't you?"

"How fortunate," replied Olivia, giving him a hug, "because I adore you."

They snuggled up on the sofa, watching breakfast television but failing to absorb any details. Suddenly, the rest of the world seemed a very distant place.

"By the way, gorgeous lady, something's given me a huge appetite. I could murder a bacon sandwich."

"Then you shall have one. I hope you like crispy bacon – I do. Maybe a fried egg on top?"

Eddie smiled – yes, she was perfect…

"I've been doing some soul-searching. I haven't had a holiday for ages so I'm taking two weeks off at the end of next month. All this Jim Foster business – coming so soon after Celia's murder – well, is getting to me, I feel drained. However, I think everything's under control, my sergeant and Angie will tie up the loose ends. The Superintendent won't say no, he's a good boss and he knows just how much unpaid overtime I do!

"Now tell me, when are you going to visit your daughter in California? Is it this autumn?"

Olivia nodded her head. Did he intend to go with her? If so, that suggested a degree of commitment. Melissa would be thrilled and proud of her. Good old mum, Eddie was quite a catch!

Eddie held her close, kissing her lovingly. He moved back in order to study her expression…

"Which of these scenarios do you prefer? A showy, autumn wedding with an expensive honeymoon in California, or, shall we get married as soon as possible and spend a week up in the Lakes, with Alan and Bertie?"

"Oh, Eddie, I can hardly believe you feel the same way. It's an easy choice – California will have to wait!

"The Hidden Tarn is so romantic: the sparkling water, the wild birds, the purple topped mountains and of course Bertie's fabulous cooking. I'm sure Alan said they have a honeymoon suite – shall we try it out?"

Eddie smiled and squeezed her hand.

"Angie thought the whole set-up was magical. She wants to go back one day – when she finds the man of her dreams – let's hope she does, she's a great girl…

The End

Epilogue

Celia's much-admired house was snapped-up by a likeable family of five...

For over twenty years Mr and Mrs Dudley had longed to move to a small rural village. Their day-dreams suggested thatched cottages, wildflower meadows, birdsong and a babbling brook. A happy, 'yet to be discovered' place where their children could thrive and grow. Sadly, the hard-working Dudley family were making little progress; they lived (or rather existed) on a run-down, crime-ridden council estate. Money was tight, the future looked bleak...

From the moment Eric Dudley promised to give up smoking their luck changed for the better...

At the end of week one (instead of being stony broke) Eric discovered the princely sum of fifty-two-pounds and sixteen pence in his bank account.

Eric was feeling jittery and short-tempered; he'd snapped at the kids which was most unusual. He'd been a smoker for over twenty years so he was bound to suffer withdrawal symptoms. He was determined, no matter how dreadful he felt, he would never smoke another cigarette. Besides, he wanted to show his mates just how much will-power he possessed! Joyce (a confirmed non-smoker) was very proud of her husband.

After he'd collected an Indian meal (to celebrate this newfound wealth) he popped into the Mini-Mart to buy sweets for the kids, packets of extra strong mints for himself and a box of chocolates for Joyce. On his way out and almost as an after-thought, he decided to splash out and treat himself to a lottery ticket.

The following Saturday, eleven people (including Eric Dudley) won the Lottery's much desired jackpot; they shared a life-changing sum of money, £36,527,000.

Eric Dudley didn't expect to be one of the winners – who does? Nothing was further from his mind; he hadn't even bothered to check his numbers. He received a phone call that made him sit down, quickly, his legs had turned to jelly. At first, he'd assumed it to be one of his workmates, young Jacko, having a laugh...

To say Joyce was thrilled would have been an understatement. At last, she could leave her mundane job on the production line at 'Leonard's Luxury Cakes and Biscuits.' She loved cooking but after working in the same factory (on-and-off) since the age of sixteen, she'd had more than enough.

Now, their wildest dreams were about to come true! They could move away from Croydon, leaving all the nastiness, worry and stress far behind them. It felt surreal, they could buy a mansion in the Cotswolds – or anywhere else they fancied! The children accepted, quite calmly, this piece of good fortune but Eric and Joyce couldn't sleep a wink – they were far too excited...

Nevertheless, Joyce had no intention of sitting at home all day, she was a busy lady who loved meeting people – perhaps she'd take on a small cafe –

there was very little she didn't know about cakes and biscuits.

Once they'd viewed and fallen in love with Celia's house, they walked the short distance to Temptations; it was certainly in a good position, right in the middle of the village. Their brand-new Mercedes was left, temporarily, in Celia's drive; no-one in this village would be dragging a key along its beautiful, shiny black paintwork.

They looked into one another's eyes their hearts full of joy; this Cotswold village fulfilled their every need. Bridgeford-upon-Avon was absolutely perfect...

"Can you believe it, girl?" whispered Eric. "Our boat's come in, alright – it's bloody magic!"

Their neighbours were in shock and green with envy. Fancy the Dudleys moving to a posh house like The Elms. Its spacious accommodation and huge lawn would get the kids from under their feet – they could play football and cricket in their very own garden! Lucky blighters!

'Just imagine it', people were saying, 'no more panicking when the rent's due.'

To top it all, Joyce would have her very own up-market cake shop. She felt nervous, would Alice and Ruby's faithful customers find fault with her cooking? Would she always be second best? Eric promised to help out in the shop, occasionally, thereby getting to know the customers. He'd try not to scoff all the profits!

"Don't you worry, babe," Joyce replied, "who needs profits? We're millionaires now!"

When Eric Dudley told Steve Hornet they wouldn't be applying for a mortgage – not for either property – it was the proudest moment of his life. Steve cheered up considerably and managed to congratulate the couple on their amazing lottery win.

Since the discovery of Lenny's decaying body, he'd been feeling depressed and despite Lenny's annoying traits, he missed him more than he cared to admit. Barnes, Hornet and Partners had been removed from their 'For Sale' signs and sadly, there was just one name displayed above the agency – Steve Hornet: Estate Agent – four lonely looking words...

With the vast amount of money from the sale of Celia's house left languishing in their bank account, Alan and Bertie had the opportunity to design a honeymoon suite with every luxury imaginable. Maybe, if they reigned it in a little, they'd be able to pay off some of their debts as well.

When Olivia and Eddie booked The Hidden Tarn for their honeymoon, Alan and Bertie felt flattered but disappointed too. This lovely couple (with whom they'd formed a firm friendship) would not be enjoying the new, deluxe honeymoon suite: there'd been several problems with planning permission. Even so, they could still give them a wonderful, romantic time. Perhaps they'd return the following year when the building work had been completed...

Bertie enjoyed trying out new recipes. He'd made a syllabub (in Celia's memory) and told Alan her recipe was the finest he'd ever tasted. Sweet sherry, plus a little fresh lemon and orange juice gave the double cream a distinctive flavour. They raised a glass to Celia, an unfulfilled and lonely woman who certainly didn't deserve to die in such a violent way.

Six months after Jim's suicide, Gallica Rose was still on the market. The purchase price had been reduced, drastically, but even so many would-be purchasers changed their minds once they became aware of its newly acquired notoriety...

Members of the public drove along the Evesham Road (at a snail's pace) gawping: others parked their cars and walked past, very slowly. What on earth were they hoping to see?

Within a matter of months Jim's delightful 18th century cottage had lost its appeal. The once cherished rear garden appeared unloved, weed-infested and abandoned.

'There's Gallica Rose, the house where the murder took place! It looks innocent enough, doesn't it? Oh, yes, Jim Foster buried the body in the back garden, under the rockery. Lenny Barnes was the local estate

agent, makes you wonder what he'd done, poor bloke. They say Mr Foster had killed before – more than once!

'Look, there's the other place, The Elms, that's where poor Celia Bamford was battered to death with an iron – not by Mr Foster, I hasten to add. Goodness me, you wouldn't want to live round here, would you?'

The tabloid newspapers hadn't helped, in fact their lurid headlines brought the wrong sort of tourists to this once peaceful village.

Bridgeford-upon-Avon

Murder Capital of England!

Perhaps, for the moment, it was... Ruby Lovegrove had murdered her twin sister, Alice, then felt obliged to 'despatch' Celia Bamford (her very good friend) simply because she'd discovered her unspeakable crime.

Cheeky Cockney, Lenny Barnes went too far when he tried to blackmail Jim Foster; he was drugged, suffocated, then buried under Jim's new rockery.

The Dudley family chose to rise above it, they knew in their hearts this was a good place to live. Eric (with his dark sense of humour) was alleged to have quipped, 'We've had a new kitchen installed at The Elms, so there's no need to worry – no bloodstains left on the kitchen floor. Anyway, just in case, my lovely wife Joyce will be doing all the ironing in the utility room!'

They weren't squeamish. Living on a run-down housing estate had toughened them up, they'd seen things that would make your hair curl...

Since Ruby's arrest, Blossom had been hiding in the garden of Mulberry cottage, surviving on mice and hand-outs from the twins' kindly neighbours. Her fur was matted and she looked underweight.

"This won't do," murmured Joyce, picking up the frightened little animal, "you're coming home with me, lovey, back to The Elms; the kids will be over the moon, they've always wanted a pet."

Joyce stood behind the counter. She was shaking her head and running out of patience...

"It's no good, Olivia, I've tried several recipes but I can't get the filling right. The pastry is lovely and light and the beef is tender but it's the gravy, there's something missing..."

"Don't you worry, Joyce, leave it with me, I've got an idea!"

Two weeks later, a small brown envelope was delivered to The Elms, Evesham Road. The stark words, Her Majesty's Prison, Easingwold, Gloucester, appeared in the top left-hand corner.

Dear Mrs Dudley,

My name is Ruby Lovegrove, no doubt you've heard of me. I murdered my identical twin sister, Alice – and our good friend Celia. There's not a day goes by when I don't regret it.

A lady from Bridgeford, called Olivia, has been writing to me, once a month, I don't deserve her kindness. Olivia mentioned the steak and ale pies, apparently you are having trouble with the filling. I have enclosed our 'secret' recipe. A bay leaf and a pinch of thyme will make all the difference. Please remember to remove the bay leaf before putting the filling in the pies!

I wish you well with Temptations, may you be as happy as we once were.

Kind Regards

Ruby Lovegrove.

The following April, shortly after Jim's house was sold and his assets liquidized, Shelly received an unexpected but very welcome letter. She'd been mentioned in Jim's will; soon, a very generous £75,000 would be transferred into her bank account. Jim knew it would enable her to enlarge and improve her salon, something she'd been longing to do…

Jim had chuckled when he told the solicitor, quite firmly, he must enclose a rather cheeky hand-written message for Shelly.

'Thank you, my darling, for making an old man very happy!' xx

The solicitor, a prudish, deeply religious and humourless man, frowned, but nevertheless carried out his client's wishes.

Every time Shelly thought of the 'real' Jim Foster – the monster lurking behind a mask of respectability – she felt unnerved and in a state of utter disbelief. Jim had murdered her ex-husband and now she would never know the reason why. Maybe he *was* a psychopath (he certainly fitted the bill) they were usually good liars and always devoid of empathy. However, it was their charm and charisma that helped them get away with murder…

Shelly felt no guilt when accepting the money, turning it down wouldn't bring back Lenny…

Her 'windfall' would be a secret (taken to the grave) even Shelly's mother would be kept in the dark. When the stunning new salon re-opened (to applause and glasses of champagne) Shelly informed her clients that she'd taken out a much bigger mortgage – she'd been advised to do so – a sensible move when interest-rates were still very low...

The remainder of Jim's fortune was split equally between three charities: Save the Children, Cancer Research and the Alzheimer's Society.

As Olivia and Eddie Logan, the Dudley family and Alan and Bertie would say:

Hold on tight to your dreams – life is full of surprises...

Printed in Great Britain
by Amazon